KT-554-595

SEASONS

SPRING

Stephanie Turnbull

 An Appleseed Editions book

First published in 2014 by Franklin Watts
338 Euston Road, London NW1 3BH

© 2012 Appleseed Editions

Created by Appleseed Editions Ltd,
Well House, Friars Hill, Guestling,
East Sussex TN35 4ET

Designed by Hel James
Edited by Mary-Jane Wilkins

All rights reserved. No part of this publication may be
reproduced, stored in a retrieval system or transmitted
in any form or by any means, electronic, mechanical,
photocopying, recording or otherwise, without prior
permission of the publisher.

A CIP record for this book is available from the
British Library

ISBN 978 1 4451 3153 5

Dewey Classification: 508.2

Photo acknowledgements
t = top, b = bottom, l = left, r = right, c = centre
page 1 DenisNata/Shutterstock; 3 iStockphoto/
Thinkstock; 5 majeczka/Shutterstock; 6 Hallgerd/
Shutterstock; 7 Ryan McVay/Thinkstock;
8 Anest/Shutterstock; 9 Smileus/Shutterstock;
10 Vishnevskiy Vasily/Shutterstock; 11t&b
iStockphoto/Thinkstock; 12b clearviewstock/
Shutterstock; 13 t&b iStockphoto/Thinkstock;
14 iStockphoto/Thinkstock; 15 visuelldesign/
Shutterstock; 16t iStockphoto/Thinkstock,
b AlessandroZocc/Shutterstock; 17 Steshkin
Yevgeniy/Shutterstock; 18b iStockphoto/
Thinkstock, c Hemera/Thinkstock; 19 Cynthia
Kidwell/Shutterstock; 20 DenisNata/Shutterstock;
21 Jenny Mie Lau King/Shutterstock; 22 t&b
3 iStockphoto/Thinkstock; 23l iStockphoto/
Thinkstock, b Hemera/Thinkstock, r Dirk Ott/
Shutterstock
Cover iStockphoto/Thinkstock

Printed in China

Franklin Watts is a division of Hachette Children's
Books, an Hachette UK company
www.hachette.co.uk

Contents

04247615

It's spring!

Bright flowers push up
through melting snow.

Sunny spring

Our spring months are March, April and May.

The sun comes up earlier every morning and sets later every evening.

Days are lighter and warmer.

Nature comes back to life after winter.

Windy weather

It is often windy in spring. This makes the weather change quickly.

One minute it is bright and breezy…

… the next minute
it is pouring
with rain!

Look for a **rainbow**
when sun shines on rain.

Time to grow

Warm spring sun and rain help new plants sprout from the soil.

Leaf buds on tree branches uncurl and *s p r e a d*.

Masses of white and pink
flowers called blossom
open on fruit trees.

Finding food

In spring, many birds fly back
from winter homes further south.
Animals wake from a long, cosy sleep.

Everyone
is hungry!

Busy bees collect
sweet nectar
from flowers.

Wiggling
worms make
tasty meals
for birds.

Here I am!

Spring can be **noisy**. Animals call and sing to each other.

Frogs puff out their throats to make deep croaks.

Birds chirp, whistle and warble.

Woodpeckers ddddrummm loudly on trees.

1

Busy builders سازندگان

Animals are soon busy making nests for babies.

Birds build nests from twigs, leaves, grass and mud.

Wasps turn
soggy bits
of wood into
papery tubes.

Eggs everywhere

Birds lay just a few eggs...

...but some animals
lay hundreds!
These are tiny
butterfly eggs.

Birds keep their eggs safe and warm until…CRACK!

Babies break out of their shells.

Lots of babies

By late spring there are babies everywhere.

Lambs can stand soon after being born. Before long they are running and jumping.

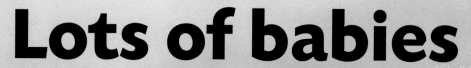

A fawn stays close to its mother and drinks her milk.

Spring fun

Many places have spring festivals to celebrate the end of winter and the start of new life.

Enjoy spring by planting seeds, spotting baby animals or hanging up nesting boxes for birds.

A cherry blossom festival in Japan.

Did you know...?

Every spring, grey whales leave warm Californian waters and swim all the way to Alaska in the far north.

When we have spring, it is autumn in the southern half of the world.

At the Indian spring festival of Holi, people throw coloured powder everywhere!

Hummingbirds lay the smallest eggs of all birds. Each egg is the size of a pea.

Useful words

bud
A bump on a branch or stem. Leaves and flowers start as buds.

fawn
A baby deer.

spring
The time of year after winter and before summer.

sprout
To begin to grow above the ground.

Index

KT-562-552

cake

recipe collection

by Sainsbury's

50 fun step-by-step decorating ideas

Welcome...

... to cake recipe collection by Sainsbury's. Inside you'll find essential information, tips and advice about making, baking and decorating cakes. With in-depth step-by-step instructions and some fantastic decorating projects for you to create at home, you'll soon be making brilliant cakes that will wow your family and friends.

Each cake has been tried, tested and tasted by Sainsbury's so you can be sure of great results every time. All the cakes are made from readily available ingredients and the decorating techniques come with easy-to-follow instructions and detailed step-by-step photography, as well as plenty of clever tips and tricks to make them easily achievable.

The book is divided into simple chapters, starting from the basics and all the cake techniques you need to know, through to brilliant cakes and cupcakes decorated for those big occasions. We hope you find plenty of inspiration to recreate these fabulous cakes.

Happy baking!

All the cakes in this book are easily achievable, however we have rated them so you can see how complex each cake is, from 🧁 for easy to 🧁 🧁 🧁 for more time-consuming decorations. For safety information, see p193.

CONTENTS

Cover cake: Mother's Day cake, **p94** **Back cover cakes:** Pirate cupcakes, **p176**

The basics

Essential equipment

To get the best baking and decorating results, you need the right tools for the job. To help, here's a glossary of baking items to consider. It's a pretty comprehensive list and you won't need all of this kit, but it will give you a good idea of some of the things you may need to create our amazing cakes. Don't forget, you'll find an array of fantastic bakeware instore or online at sainsburys.co.uk to help you make and decorate the cakes in this book.

■ Measuring

When baking, it's vital that you measure ingredients accurately for the cakes to work

Scales
Essential for weighing dry ingredients such as flour and sugar. Consider an electronic version for spot-on accuracy.

Measuring jug
For measuring liquids and identifying the volume of unmarked bowls (just fill with water and pour back into a measuring jug).

Measuring spoons
For accurate measurement of small quantities of ingredients such as baking powder or vanilla extract.

■ Mixing

To get the right fluffy consistency for your cakes, you'll need the correct mixing tools

Electric food mixer
A stand mixer takes the hard work out of creaming your mixture; different attachments will cover a range of tasks.

Electric hand whisk
Use an electric hand whisk to cream cake and icing mixtures, as well as beating eggs and whipping cream.

Wooden spoons
If you don't have a mixer or hand whisk, then you'll need a good wooden spoon and plenty of elbow grease!

Spatula
Designed for scraping every last bit of mixture from your bowl and good for levelling the cake's surface before baking.

Sieve
Sifting ingredients such as flour helps to get rid of lumps and adds a little more air to your cake mixture.

Mixing bowls
No baker can be without a set of these. For most baking jobs, you'll need one large and one small.

■ Baking

Prepare for baking and beyond with these essentials

Baking paper
A good lining of baking paper will help make sure your cakes don't stick to their tins (see p20 for how to line your tins).

Cupcake and muffin cases
Paper cases come in a range of designs. The trick is never to fill more than two-thirds full, as the mixture will expand during baking.

Cake tester or skewer
To see if your cake is cooked, insert a cake tester or skewer into the centre. If it comes out clean, it's done.

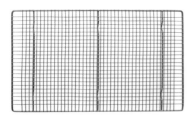

Wire rack
A good wire rack is essential, allowing air to circulate and your cakes to cool quickly and evenly, ready for you to decorate them.

Rectangular tin
Many of the cakes in this book are baked in rectangular tins, the perfect starting point for cutting out different shapes.

Muffin tin
To make cupcakes and muffins you'll need a muffin tin. You'll normally need paper cupcake or muffin cases, too (see above).

Round tin
Check the individual recipes to find out what size round tins you'll need for your chosen decorating project.

Loaf tin
Loaf tins usually come in 1lb (450g) and 2lb (900g) sizes. They're usually used for bread baking but are perfect for cakes, too.

Square tin
Square tins come in a variety of different sizes and, like round tins, are essential for every keen cake baker.

■ Decorating
Here's what you'll need to add your finishing touches

Cutters
Cutters are available in a huge range of fun shapes - you'll use them for cutting out cake as well as biscuit and icing shapes.

Palette knife
A palette knife is the perfect tool for creating smooth buttercream icing surfaces and helping to ease cakes out of tins.

Cake smoother/edger
This tool gives a professional finish to soft icing, quickly smoothing out lumps and pleats, and creating a lovely shine.

Cake board
Use a cake board for beautiful presentation or as a handy surface to work on while you're decorating your cake.

Rolling pin
It's ideal for rolling soft icing, but a rolling pin is also the perfect tool to help you pick up and lay icing on your cake.

Serrated knife
It's the only knife to use for shaping or cutting cakes (see p21 for details on how to achieve a professional finish).

Icing modelling kit
These little tools are specially made for crafting soft icing or marzipan into intricate shapes.

Icing bag and nozzles
Disposable icing bags and a set of nozzles in different sizes are essential for piping icing onto your cakes.

Pastry and fine paint brushes
Use these for applying glaze, glacé or other types of icing or for dabbing on a little water to stick on flowers and other decorations.

Baking
essentials...

For baking perfection, use the best ingredients you can find!

Fruit and nuts

Fruit cake recipes call for a variety of dried fruits, including sultanas, currants, raisins, apricots, dates and tropical fruits. Nuts are included in some recipes, too – either ground, flaked, chopped or whole – for added flavour and texture.

Eggs

Eggs add volume and a lighter texture to your cake mixture. Make sure you have the right size for the recipe, and take them out of the fridge at least 2 hours before they're needed to prevent curdling when you start to mix.

Baking powder

Cakes need raising agents in order to rise, and adding baking powder to flour is one way to achieve a great result.

Flour
Self-raising flour has baking powder already added for convenience. Plain flour does not contain baking powder, but it can be added as needed to give cakes the correct rise. We've used self-raising flour in our basic cake recipes with added baking powder for extra lift.

Flavourings
You can add a number of flavours to a basic sponge recipe. Cocoa powder (as pictured), vanilla extract, citrus extract, zest and juice all add a distinctive taste to an otherwise plain cake.

Sugar
Sugar is a baking and decorating staple, and you'll find a huge variety on offer, from icing, caster and granulated to demerara, and light and dark soft brown sugar. Fine white or golden caster sugar are used in most cake baking recipes.

Butter
Unsalted is best for baking. Unless a recipe says otherwise, make sure it's at room temperature to make mixing easier.

Best before end:

The basic cakes

All of the cakes in this book use one of three of the following basic mixtures – for Victoria sponge, chocolate sponge or fruit cake. The quantities and tin sizes you'll need are given at the beginning of each cake recipe, along with individual cooking times. There's also a recipe for a basic biscuit dough, which is used to make decorations for some of the cakes.

Victoria sponge

For 1 quantity of Victoria sponge mixture, you will need:

250g unsalted butter, softened, plus extra for greasing

250g white caster sugar

1 tsp vanilla extract

4 large eggs, beaten

250g self-raising flour

1/2 tsp baking powder

1 Preheat the oven to 180°C, fan 160°C, gas 4. Grease your cake tin or tins (see individual cake recipes for sizes), then line with baking parchment (see p20).

2 In a large mixing bowl, use an electric hand whisk to cream together the butter, sugar and vanilla extract until light and fluffy.

3 Beat in the eggs one at a time, adding a little flour with each egg to stop the mixture splitting.

4 Sift over the remaining flour and baking powder, then gently fold in with a wooden spoon until the mixture is smooth.

5 Put the mixture into the tin or tins (divide the mixture equally between tins if using more than one; if you want to be exact, weigh the mixture). Bake in the preheated oven for the time stated on each cake recipe. The cake is cooked when a skewer inserted into the middle comes out clean. It should be golden and risen, and spring back to the touch.

6 Turn the cake out onto a wire rack and allow to cool completely before you start decorating.

Top tip
To make a lemon-flavoured sponge, mix the grated zest of 2 lemons and the juice of 1 into the mixture before adding the flour.

Chocolate sponge

For 1 quantity of chocolate sponge mixture, you will need:

250g unsalted butter, softened, plus extra for greasing

75g cocoa powder

50ml sunflower oil

400g white caster sugar

1 tsp vanilla extract

4 medium eggs

300g self-raising flour

1 tsp baking powder

1 Preheat the oven to 180°C, fan 160°C, gas 4. Grease a cake tin or tins (see individual cake recipes for sizes), then line with baking parchment (see p20). In a small bowl, whisk the cocoa powder into 125ml boiling water. Stir in the sunflower oil, then set aside to cool slightly.

2 In a large mixing bowl, use an electric hand whisk to cream together the butter, sugar and vanilla extract until light and fluffy.

3 Beat in the eggs one at a time, adding a little of the flour with each egg to stop the mixture splitting. Beat in the cocoa mixture.

4 Sift over the remaining flour and baking powder, then gently fold in with a wooden spoon until the mixture is smooth.

5 Put the mixture into the prepared tin or tins (divide the mixture equally between tins if using more than one; if you want to be exact, weigh the mixture). Bake in the preheated oven for the time specified on the cake recipe. The cake is cooked when a skewer inserted into the middle comes out clean. It should be risen and spring back to the touch.

6 Turn out onto a wire rack and allow to cool completely before you start decorating.

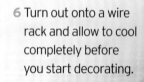

Storage and freezing

Once cool, sponge cakes can be wrapped in cling film or placed in an airtight container for up to 3 days. They can also be frozen: set aside until fully cooled, wrap in cling film, put in an airtight container and freeze for up to 1 month. Defrost thoroughly then continue using as you would a fresh cake. Once decorated, the cakes will keep for a further 3 days.

Fruit cake

For 1 quantity of fruit cake mixture, you will need:

200g unsalted butter, softened, plus extra for greasing

200g dark brown soft sugar

2 tbsp black treacle

Grated zest of 1 lemon

Juice and grated zest of 1 orange

4 medium eggs, lightly beaten

225g plain flour, sifted

1 tsp mixed spice

1kg mixed fruit

100g glacé cherries, halved

100g blanched almonds, chopped

3-4 tbsp brandy

1 Preheat the oven to 150°C, fan 130°C, gas 2. Grease a cake tin or tins (see individual cake recipes for the number and size of tins you'll need), then line with baking parchment (see p20).

2 In a large mixing bowl, use an electric hand whisk to cream together the butter and sugar, then mix in the treacle, lemon zest, orange juice and zest.

3 Gradually mix in the eggs until combined, then fold in the flour and spice. Stir in the fruit, cherries and almonds.

4 Put the mixture in the prepared tin or tins. Wrap a double layer of brown paper around the outside of the tin or tins, securing with string, then cover the top/s with another layer of brown paper with a diamond shape cut out of the middle (see p21).

5 Bake for the time specified in the cake recipe. A skewer inserted into the middle of the cake should come out clean. If not, return the cake to the oven for a further 20-30 mins.

6 Remove from the oven and cool in the tin for 15 mins. Turn out onto a wire rack and leave to cool completely.

7 Once cool, make a few holes in the cake with a skewer and drizzle over the brandy (you may want to 'feed' your cake with more brandy every week until you are ready to ice it).

Storage and freezing

Wrap the cooled fruit cake in baking parchment and keep in an airtight box. It can be 'fed' with 1 tbsp brandy every few weeks. It will keep for up to 2 months. To freeze: set aside until fully cooled, wrap in cling film or put in an airtight container and freeze for up to 6 months. Defrost fully then continue using as you would a freshly baked cake. Once decorated, it will keep for a further 2 months.

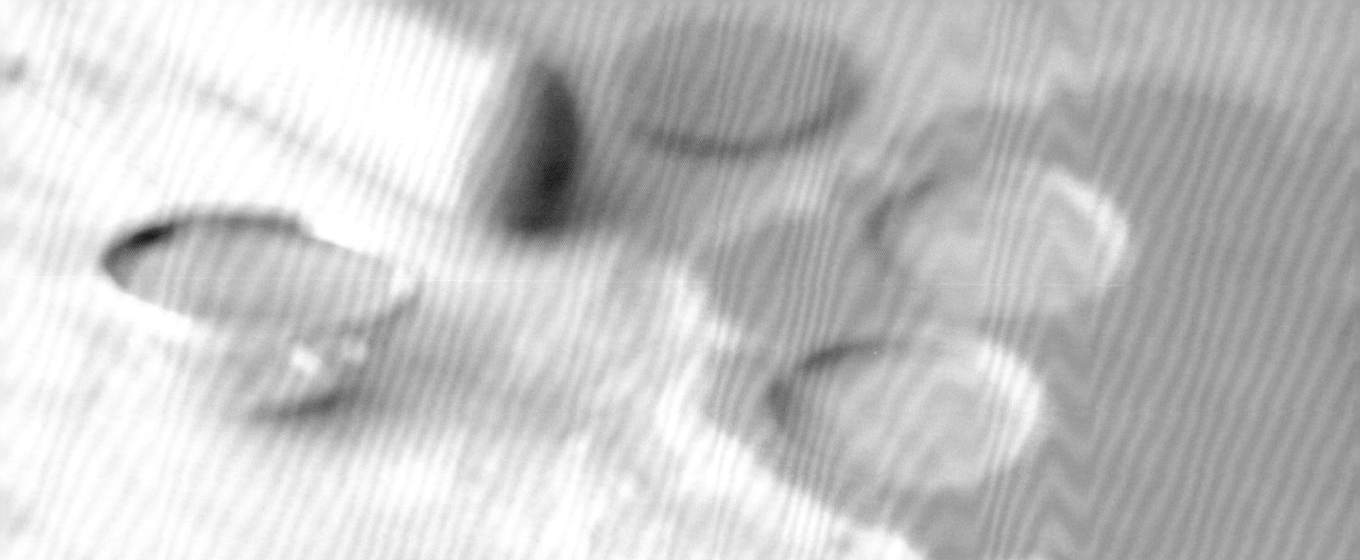

Biscuits

To make around 20-30 biscuits, you will need:

200g unsalted butter, softened

200g white caster sugar

1 medium egg, lightly beaten

400g plain flour, plus extra for dusting

1 In a large mixing bowl, use an electric whisk to cream the butter with the sugar until well mixed and just creamy in texture. Do not overwork, or the biscuits will spread during baking.

2 Beat in the egg until well combined, then gather the dough into a ball, wrap in cling film and chill for at least 1 hour.

3 Preheat the oven to 190°C, fan 170°C, gas 5. Put the dough on a lightly floured surface and knead briefly, then roll out to 3mm thick. Cut, by hand or with cookie cutters, to your desired shapes (see the individual recipes for details). Using a palette knife, transfer the biscuits to a baking tray lined with baking parchment.

4 Bake for 12-14 mins, depending on the size of your biscuits, until golden brown at the edges. Remove from the oven and transfer to a wire rack to cool.

Storage and freezing
If you don't need all of the dough, you can wrap the rest in cling film and keep in the fridge for up to 3 days or freeze for up to 3 months. To use, defrost fully overnight in the fridge and continue from step 3.

How to prepare tins

To stop your cakes sticking, it's worth spending a little time lining your tins

Round tins

Grease the inside of the tin with oil or melted butter. Place on a sheet of baking paper and draw around the base with a pencil. Cut out the circle and use to line the tin's base.

Measure the circumference of the tin with string. Cut a sheet of baking paper to this length and just over the height of the tin; line the tin, smoothing it against the side.

Rectangular/square tins

Cut a piece of baking paper big enough to line your tin. At an angle, cut in to each corner of the parchment. Grease the tin and line with the parchment, letting it overlap at the corners.

Fruit cake tins

Line the tin with baking paper as before. Sit the filled tin on a double layer of brown paper, pull the sides up around the cake and secure with string. Tuck in another sheet of paper on top with a hole cut in the middle.

How to cut and fill cakes

These simple tricks will give your creations a professional finish

Trimming cake tops

If the surface of your cake needs to be totally flat, use a long serrated knife (such as a bread knife) to trim the top of the cake. Slowly and evenly cut horizontally from one side to the other, using a gentle sawing motion, with the palm of your hand resting lightly on the surface of the cake.

Cutting and filling cakes for the best results

One of the secrets to a beautifully even cake is accurate, clean cutting and placement. Here's how to do it

Place your cooled cake on a chopping board. With a long serrated knife, using a gentle sawing motion, cut carefully through the cake horizontally, with the palm of your hand resting lightly on top of the cake. Insert a cocktail stick 1cm above the cut on the top half and 1cm below the cut on the bottom half. Make sure the cocktail sticks are aligned vertically.

Remove the top half of the cake and carefully spoon your buttercream filling over the bottom half of the cake. Smooth it out gently. Place the top half of the cake on the buttercream, making sure that the two cocktail sticks are aligned vertically once more to give you an even finish. Remove the cocktail sticks and continue to decorate your cake.

Icings and frostings

All the cakes in this book will require icing or frosting of some sort.
The ingredients used here amount to 1 quantity in the cake recipes

■ Glacé icing

A smooth, glossy icing created by simply mixing icing sugar and water. Its thin consistency makes it perfect for drizzling over large cakes, fairy cakes, tarts and buns. Glacé icing can be easily coloured and flavoured.

4 tbsp icing sugar

1 In a small bowl mix together the icing sugar with about 1 tsp water until you have a thin, smooth icing. For a thicker consistency add another tablespoon of icing sugar.

Tip: This makes quite a small amount. However, you can easily increase the icing sugar and add more liquid to achieve the consistency you want. For flavoured glacé icing, replace the water with fresh fruit juices, such as lemon, orange or lime.

■ Vanilla buttercream

A simple, all-purpose icing with a soft, buttery texture that's perfect as a filling or topping for all kinds of cakes. It can also be coloured and flavoured in lots of different ways (see panel opposite). Pipe it in thick swirls for a really decadent finish.

250g unsalted butter, at room temperature
1 tsp vanilla extract
500g icing sugar

1 In a large mixing bowl, use an electric hand whisk to beat together the butter and vanilla extract for 2-3 mins, until pale and soft.

2 Add half the icing sugar and beat on a low setting at first, so the icing sugar doesn't puff up and out of your bowl. Beat on a higher setting until smooth, then repeat with the rest of the icing sugar. Continue to beat for 1-2 mins, until pale and fluffy.

3 To colour the buttercream, beat in a little food colouring. If you're using liquid food colouring, take care not to add too much as it will make the buttercream looser. If you want a deeper colour, it's better to use food colourings in gel or paste form.

Tip: If you are piping buttercream rather than using it as a filling or topping, loosen the mixture with a couple of teaspoons of milk.

■ Chocolate ganache

A shiny, fudge-like icing that's very rich and deliciously gooey! When it's still warm, ganache can be poured over cakes, or spread or piped when chilled. You can also combine it with buttercream for a decadent filling.

150ml double cream
150g dark chocolate, broken up

1 Put the double cream in a pan and gently heat until a few bubbles are showing, but it is not fully boiling.

2 Remove from the heat and add the dark chocolate, stirring until fully melted.

3 Allow to cool, then place in the fridge for 10 mins until the ganache is a thick but spreadable consistency.

Buttercream flavour variations

Quick chocolate Add 2 tbsp cocoa powder to the buttercream with the icing sugar and mix until smooth and fully combined.

Rich chocolate Stir 100g melted and slightly cooled chocolate (see p25) – you can use white, milk or dark – through the finished buttercream.

Orange Beat the zest of 2 oranges into the finished buttercream.

Lemon Beat the zest of 1 lemon and 3 tbsp lemon curd into the finished buttercream.

Strawberry Beat 4 tbsp strawberry jam and 1/2 tsp pink food colouring into the finished buttercream.

*Public health advice is to avoid consumption of raw or lightly cooked eggs, especially those vulnerable to infection, including pregnant women, babies and the elderly.

■ Royal icing

Traditionally used for covering special occasion cakes, royal icing, which dries to a hard paste, is now used more for cake decoration and intricate piping of decorations such as flowers, borders and letters. This quick recipe uses a ready-made mix to make it really easy.

500g royal icing sugar

1 Combine the royal icing and 80ml cold water in a deep bowl. Using an electric mixer or electric hand whisk, starting slowly and gradually increasing the speed, beat for about 5 mins, until standing in soft peaks. If the icing is too soft, beat in a little icing sugar, a teaspoon at a time. Add a few drops of water if it is too stiff.

Tip: To make the same amount of royal icing from scratch, put 2 medium egg whites* into a mixing bowl and whisk until soft peaks form. Stir in 2 tsp lemon juice, then gradually beat in 500g icing sugar until the icing drops off the spoon and holds its trail for 10 secs.

■ Cream cheese frosting

This quick and easy frosting is perfect for many afternoon tea favourites, including a classic carrot cake. Its thick, stable consistency makes it a great all-rounder, ideal for piping, spreading or layering. Create a richer taste with a touch of orange zest, or spice it up with a dusting of ground cinnamon.

200g unsalted butter, softened

200g icing sugar

200g soft cream cheese

1 In a large mixing bowl, use an electric hand whisk to beat the butter for 2-3 mins, until pale and soft.

2 Add in half of the icing sugar and beat on a low setting at first, so that the icing sugar doesn't all puff up and out of your bowl. Beat on a higher setting until smooth, then repeat with the other half of the icing. Continue to beat for 1-2 mins, until the mixture is fluffy and pale.

3 Finish by beating in the cream cheese until smooth.

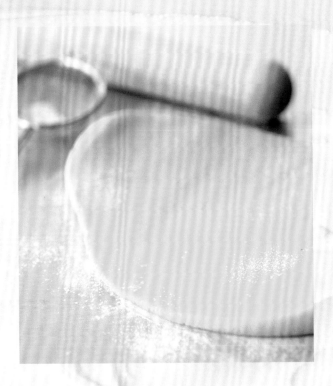

■ Marzipan

Made from ground almonds, sugar and egg, marzipan can be used in a whole host of ways. As a covering for fruit cakes, it helps them retain moisture and provides a smooth base for icing. Use a ready-made pack (as pictured) to save time or make this version:

200g ground almonds

75g caster sugar

150g icing sugar

1/2 tsp almond essence

1 large egg*, beaten

1 Put the almonds and caster sugar in a food processor and pulse until you have a fine crumb. Pour into a bowl and mix in the icing sugar and almond essence.

2 Using a knife, stir the egg into the mixture. When it forms a clump, turn out onto a surface dusted with icing sugar and knead to a smooth dough, but don't overwork. Wrap in cling film and keep in a cool place for up to 2 days until ready to use.

How to... melt chocolate

Place a pan of water over a low heat. Bring to a gentle simmer and place a heatproof bowl over the top, making sure it doesn't touch the water – the heat should come from the steam only. Break up the chocolate, add to the bowl and let it slowly melt. Stir gently once or twice. You don't want the chocolate to burn, so when nearly all the chocolate has melted, remove from the heat and stir constantly until completely melted.

How to roll and apply icing

A layer of soft icing creates a nice even base for cake decorating. This simple guide will help you get it right every time

For most of the cakes in this book, the decorating starts with a layer of soft icing to give you a smooth, even surface to work on. To keep things simple, we've used Sainsbury's ready to roll icing. Buying ready made icing is much easier than making soft icing from scratch and you'll save yourself a lot of time and effort. Sainsbury's ready to roll soft icing comes in white, ivory, chocolate, plus a range of different colours. If you like, you can create your own colours using white ready to roll icing and food colouring. Simply knead the food colouring into the icing, a drop at a time, until the colour is evenly spread throughout.

Our simple step-by-step guide to rolling and applying icing will help you to achieve the best, most professional-looking results.

1 Each recipe tells you how much icing you will need but, as a general guide, 500g is usually enough to cover a 15cm-18cm round cake. Cold icing is tricky to work with, so don't keep it in the fridge. Begin by kneading the icing for a minute or two until it is softer and more pliable. If it gets too warm, it may become sticky, so stop kneading as soon as it's pliable.

2 Lightly dust your work surface with a small amount of icing sugar. With a rolling pin, begin to roll out the kneaded ball of icing, applying an even pressure. Give the icing a quarter turn every so often to retain a nice circular shape. Continue rolling until the icing is the thickness specified in the decorating instructions.

3 Cover your cake with a thin layer of buttercream or spread on a glaze of apricot jam (or buy apricot glaze by Sainsbury's) that has been gently warmed through. This will ensure the icing sticks to your cake.

4 Use a rolling pin to help you lift the icing. Drape the sheet of icing over the cake, making sure it is positioned centrally.

5 Keeping your hands flat, gently smooth the icing over the top of the cake, pressing it over the edges, smoothing it down the sides and gently easing out any pleats. For a professional finish, dust a cake smoother/edger with icing sugar and glide it in a circular motion all over the cake.

6 Trim off the excess icing from around the base of the cake with a sharp knife. If you have time, let the icing dry in a cool place overnight before moving on to the next step of cake decorating.

How to pipe icing

Beautifully piped icing can transform a cake from simple to simply sensational. And it's easier than you might think. Our beginners' guide, a steady hand and a little practise are all you need to impress

Basic piping technique

1 Snip off the end of a disposable piping bag, using your chosen nozzle as a guide (the hole should be about the same width as the nozzle halfway up). Fit the nozzle in the bag, taking care that it doesn't catch inside the bag.

2 Fold down the top of the piping bag over your hand to make it smaller and more manageable – this will make it much easier to fill with icing. Spoon the icing into the bag.

3 Unfold the top, gather it with one hand and gently squeeze down towards the nozzle, holding the nozzle end with the other hand, until the icing is about to start coming out. This removes any air from the icing, helping it to come out evenly and smoothly. Twist the top of the bag a few times to create pressure behind the icing.

4 Hold the top of the bag with your writing hand and cradle the nozzle end in your other hand. Position the nozzle on the cake and squeeze the icing from the top until it starts coming out. Keep the pressure even and the nozzle moving. To finish, stop squeezing and push the nozzle slightly towards the cake, then draw back to break the flow of icing. It may help to practise on a plate before you start.

How to pipe writing/shapes

Ideal for: cakes with a message
Use: a writing piping nozzle

With a cocktail stick, make small holes in the surface of the cake to outline the words or the shape you wish to make (you can use mini cutters to get the right shape, see right). Fill a piping bag fitted with a writing nozzle (see p30-31) with icing or room-temperature melted chocolate (see p25). Practise writing on a plate or sheet of baking paper. When you're feeling confident, pipe onto the cake following the outline you made with the cocktail stick. Use your non-writing hand to hold the nozzle end of the bag as steady as possible so the icing comes out evenly.

How to pipe dots

Ideal for: decorative designs
Use: a round piping nozzle

Hold the piping bag vertically, placing the nozzle close to the cake. Squeeze out a little icing to make the dot. To finish, push the bag down and draw up quickly.

How to pipe swirls

Ideal for: perfect party cupcakes
Use: a large star-shaped piping nozzle

Hold the bag vertically, then pipe a ring around the edge of the cupcake. Pipe a spiral inside the ring, slightly overlapping it – stop squeezing when you reach the centre of the cake. To finish, push the bag down slightly and draw up quickly.

Your essential piping kit

You can find piping sets instore that include the piping bag and a selection of different sized and shaped nozzles for creating various icing effects. The cakes in this book use disposable plastic piping bags by Sainsbury's, which you can cut to fit whatever nozzles you have. For finer details and for writing messages, little tubes of ready-to-go writing icing pens by Sainsbury's come in a range of colours, and are a quick and easy choice.

Piping tips

• If you're a beginner at piping writing, try using a joined-up script rather than individual letters – you'll be able to keep up a continuous flow, instead of having to keep stopping and starting.

• When piping with a fine nozzle, you may need to thicken your royal icing a little using a few teaspoons of icing sugar. Experiment until you discover the consistency that works best for you.

• To pipe simple patterns or shapes, such as stars or flowers use the cocktail stick technique (see above) or lightly press a cookie cutter into the icing, then use the impression as your piping guide.

Large star
Perfect for piping thick, rich swirls of buttercream icing onto the top of cupcakes

Writing
Personalise your cakes with a name or a greeting, but make sure you practise first!

Know your nozzles

Whether you need a star shaped, round or writing piping nozzle, using the right tool for the job will make all the difference. Here's our quick guide

Small star
Closely packed rosettes make
a pretty cupcake topping or
edging to a larger cake

Round
Ideal for piping stripes,
borders, spots and scrolls on
larger cakes and on cupcakes

Fine writing
Brilliant for writing
messages on
smaller cakes or
for stripes, swirls
and lacework

How to make decorative flowers and figures

A trail of handcrafted leaves, a family of ducks or a copse of Nordic firs really are the icing on the cake. And they're surprisingly easy when you know how

Once you have your icing base, you can use various decorating techniques to customise your cake. You can make almost any shape, from simple flowers to elaborate characters, and experiment with different ideas. These designs are for specific cakes but, once you've gained a little confidence, you'll find they lend themselves to adaptation, too.

Making flowers and leaves

Making decorative flowers and leaves are a staple of classic cake decorating and an enjoyable way to add a pretty finish to your cake. They can be made in an array of different colours and styles, so it's easy to personalise your creation.

Leaves and flowers
(Simple Christmas cake, p112)

Icing sugar, for dusting
60g ready to roll white icing
Leaf, ivy, flower and leaf cutters
1/2 tsp green food colouring
1 fine paint brush
1 tsp white shimmer pearls by Sainsbury's
30g ready to roll green icing
2 tsp red pearls (optional, from 69g pot red, blue and white pearls by Sainsbury's)

1 Dust a work surface with icing sugar and roll out the white icing to 3mm thick. Stamp out ivy, leaves and flowers or cut them out by hand.

2 Paint the ivy leaves with a little green food colouring, then mark on veins by gently scoring with a knife. Paint the centre of the flowers with a little green food colouring and, once dry, use cooled boiled water to stick a few white shimmer pearls to the centre of each flower. Let the flowers and leaves dry in the holes of an egg box or in egg cups, so that the edges curl up slightly. Leave them to dry out in a cool place for 3-4 hours or overnight.

3 Dust a work surface with icing sugar and roll out the green icing to 3mm thick. Cut out leaves either by hand (about 4cm in length) or with a cutter. Mark on the veins by gently scoring with a knife, then dry over a rolling pin to give a gentle curve to the leaves.

4 Use the leaves and flowers to decorate your cake, attaching with a little cooled boiled water. Attach the red pearl 'berries' in the same way, at the base of the leaves.

Icing bow
(Surprise cake, p46)

60g ready to roll yellow icing

1 Roll out the icing to 3mm thick. Trim to a 5cm x 15cm strip. Reserve the trimmings.

2 Brush cooled boiled water along the centre and ends of the strip. Fold in from both ends to meet in the centre. Pinch together at the centre to make a bow.

3 Roll and cut a thin strip of icing from the trimmings and secure over the pinched section with a little cooled boiled water.

4 Slide the handles of 2 wooden spoons between the loops of the bow.

5 Leave to dry in a cool place for 2-3 hours before removing the wooden spoons.

Making figures
If you enjoyed playing with modelling clay as a child, you'll love making these fun icing figures!

Rubber duck
(New baby cake, p134)

50g ready to roll yellow icing
3g ready to roll orange icing
1 cocktail stick
Black writing icing pen (from 76g pack colour writing icing by Sainsbury's)

1 For the body, roll 30g of the yellow icing into a slightly flattened oval with a point at one end. Roll a 10g piece into a ball for the head.

2 Use 2 x 5g pieces for the wings. Roll into 2 ovals, then flatten and make a point at one end.

3 Roll the orange icing into a beak shape, mark in the mouth with a cocktail stick, then stick all the parts together using a little cooled boiled water to secure. Mark the duck's eyes with the black writing icing pen.

Teddy bear
(New baby cake, p134)

65g ready to roll blue icing
Black writing icing pen (from 76g pack
colour writing icing by Sainsbury's)
1 cocktail stick

1   Use 30g of icing for the body and
    a 12g piece for the head. Roll into
    an oval shape for the body and
    a ball for the head and set aside.
    Use 2 x 5g pieces of icing for the legs
    - roll into long sausage shapes, leaving
    one end slightly thicker for the feet.
    Use 2 x 3g pieces for the arms and roll into
    sausage shapes.

2   Roll a small amount of icing into an oval
    for the snout. Roll 2 tiny pieces of icing into
    balls for the ears, then flatten and shape
    around a cocktail stick.

3   Stick the parts together using cooled
    boiled water to secure. Mark on the eyes
    and nose using the black writing icing pen.

Snowman
(Christmas house cake, p114)

40g ready to roll white icing
8g ready to roll black icing
10g ready to roll red icing
Black writing icing pen (from 76g pack
colour writing icing by Sainsbury's)

1   Roll 25g of white icing into a ball for the
    body; roll 10g into a ball for the head. For
    the hat, roll 5g of black icing into a ball,
    then gently flatten to a cylinder. Roll the
    remaining black icing into a ball, then
    flatten to a disc for the brim of the hat. For
    the scarf, roll 8g red icing into a long thin
    sausage shape and set aside.

2   Stick all the parts together using a little
    cooled boiled water to secure. Mark the
    eyes, mouth and buttons with the black
    writing icing pen. To finish, mix a tiny
    amount of red and white icing together
    and roll into a ball for the nose.

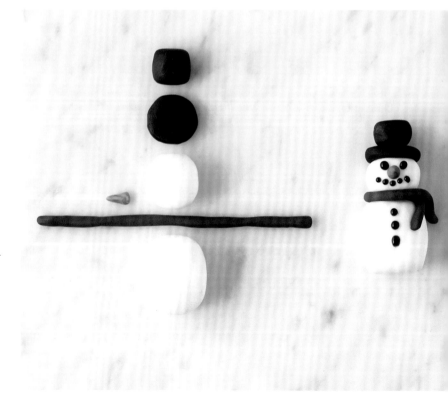

Golf bag and accessories
(Golf lover's cake, p148)

50g ready to roll red icing
15g ready to roll white icing
1 cocktail stick

1 For the main part of the bag, roll 35g of red icing into a slightly rounded and flattened rectangle. Roll and flatten a 5g piece for the pocket, then roll a 10g piece of red icing into a sausage shape and cut a strip for the golf bag handle.

2 Make the golf clubs using the white icing: roll into 4 thin sausage shapes, each about 2cm in length. Make one end slightly thicker and bend it to a 90° angle.

3 Stick all the parts of the bag together, with the golf clubs protruding from the top of the bag, using a little cooled boiled water to secure in place. Mark detail on the golf bag pocket and around the top of the bag using a cocktail stick.

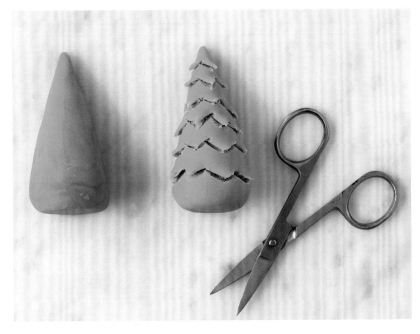

Fir tree
(Christmas house cake, p114, and Golf lover's cake, p148)

40g ready to roll green icing

1 Roll the icing into a cone shape. Using small scissors and, starting at the base of the cone, make little cuts into the icing in rows, working all the way up.

Top tip
Ready to roll icing dries out quickly once it's out of the pack and will soon become hard to model. To keep it pliable and soft, don't use too much icing sugar and cover any pieces you're not working with in cling film.

Decorating ingredients

There is a huge selection of colourful, fun decorating ingredients available that can help you create cakes that look as good as they taste – and you can use them in all sorts of creative ways. Look out for them in the home baking aisle at your local Sainsbury's store.

◼ Sprinkles

From traditional 100s & 1000s to chocolate sprinkles and patriotic red, white and blue pearls, sprinkles and sparkles will add instant colour to any cake.

Top tip: When sprinkling, sit your cake on a wire rack, then put the rack into a large baking tray that's been lined with baking parchment. That way, all the sprinkles that don't make it onto the cake can easily be recycled – see the Surprise cake on p46.

◼ Shapes and figures

From little flowers and stars to heart-shaped confetti, ready-made shapes are a quick way to add a professional-looking touch to cupcakes or larger creations. Most are made from either sugar or chocolate.

Top tip: Sometimes, more is more! Group a few little stars, hearts or flowers together on a cupcake for maximum effect. Try our Garden lover's cake on p144.

◼ Chocolates and sweets

As a one-off treat, there's no easier way to delight a birthday boy or girl than to present them with a cake laden with sweets. Use chocolate chips, marshmallows, chocolate coins, liquorice laces and different jelly sweets to create all sorts of irresistible effects.

Top tip: If you need to cut sweets, such as marshmallows or liquorice into different shapes or sizes for your cake design (for an example, see our Pig cake on p78), don't use a knife - a pair of good kitchen scissors will make the job much quicker and easier.

◼ Lustres and glitters

Add a touch of glamour to a grown-up cake with edible lustres, glitter sugar and gold or silver balls. These look especially effective on a background of dark chocolate ganache.

Top tip: A little bit of lustre dust goes a long way. The dry powder can be brushed straight onto icing decorations with a small paint brush, or, for a more intense effect, mix the dust with a few drops of vodka or an alcohol-based flavouring such as lemon essence, then paint it on. See our Ruffle wedding cake on p124 for what you can achieve.

◼ Writing icing

If you're not totally confident of your piping skills, writing icing is your saviour. Available in a range of different flavours and colours, including glitter-effect varieties, they're simple to use and mess-free, so perfect if the kids are helping out. See our Halloween graveyard cake on p102.

Top tip: As well as spelling out words or names, writing icing is great for detailed work such as swirls and scrolls. See our Spider's web cupcakes on p166.

◼ Dried fruit and nuts

What could be a more classic cake decoration than the glacé cherry? Dried fruit and nuts, such as flaked almonds, walnut halves, desiccated coconut, crystallised ginger and freeze-dried raspberries and strawberries not only look appealing, but they also add another level of flavour to your cakes.

Top tip: Desiccated coconut gives a fantastic nutty flavour - see our Panda cupcakes on p170 and our Bunny cake on p42.

◼ Ribbons and decorative picks

For pretty finishing touches, add colourful ribbons and decorative picks (such as princess cupcake picks by Sainsbury's). There are even silver paper frills to dress up cupcakes.

Top tip: A simple band of ribbon tied around the bottom of a cake looks stylish and understated - see our Simple Christmas cake on p112 or our Golf lover's cake on p148.

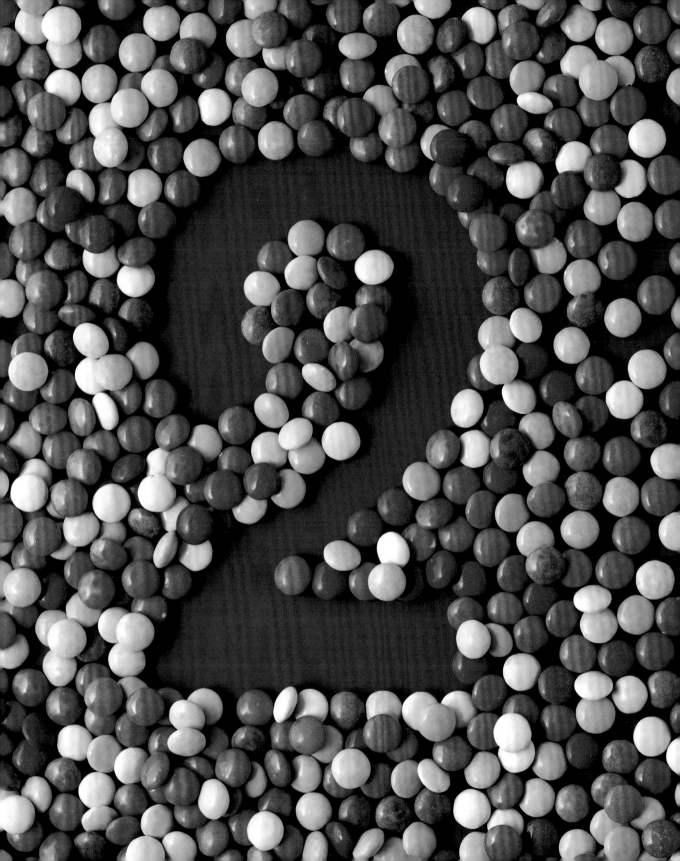

Cakes for kids

Flower cake

Make her feel like a princess with this gorgeous girlie birthday cake

RATING

SERVES 16

YOU WILL NEED
1 quantity vanilla buttercream (see p22)

1 quantity Victoria sponge mixture baked in 2 x 15cm round deep cake tins for 45 mins (see p14), cooled

1 quantity glacé icing (see p22)

TO DECORATE
1 tsp pink food colouring

10 tbsp strawberry jam

Icing sugar, for dusting

250g pack ready to roll green icing by Sainsbury's

75g ready to roll yellow icing

75g ready to roll white icing

Black writing icing pen (from 76g pack colour writing icing by Sainsbury's)

1 x pack mini blossom cake decorations by Sainsbury's

A few drops of blue food colouring

YOU WILL ALSO NEED
25cm round cake board

Mini heart-shaped and teardrop-shaped cookie cutters (from mini cookie cutter set by Sainsbury's)

1 fine paint brush

1 disposable piping bag

1 star-shaped piping nozzle

Birthday candles

PER SERVING
647 cals, 29.7g fat, 16.9g sat fat, 77.9g total sugars, 0.22g salt

1 Put the buttercream in a large bowl and add the pink food colouring. Mix well to combine.

2 Trim the tops of the cakes to create flat surfaces (picture A, see p21). Sandwich the cakes with the jam and a quarter of the buttercream. Spread a quarter of the remaining buttercream all over the cake. Put on the board and chill for 10 mins. Use half of the remaining buttercream to apply a second layer. Transfer to the fridge to chill.

3 To make the grass, dust a surface with icing sugar and roll out the green icing to 3mm thick. Cut out a strip from the icing (about 50cm x 10cm) to fit around the base of the cake. Along one side, use a sharp knife to create a jagged grass effect. Cut into sections, then press along the bottom of the cake (picture B).

4 To make the bees, dust a surface with icing sugar and roll out the yellow and white icings to 2mm thick. Cut out 10 white icing hearts and 10 yellow teardrops with the cutters. Brush with glacé icing, then place a heart shape at an angle on the teardrop 'body' and press to secure. Repeat with the others. Finish by piping on the bees' stripes and eyes with black writing icing. Brush glacé icing on the underside of the bees and blossoms and stick onto the cake.

5 Divide the remaining buttercream between 2 bowls. Add a little of the blue colouring to 1 bowl to make a light purple. Place alternate spoonfuls of pink and purple buttercream in a piping bag with a star nozzle. Pipe roses around the outside of the top of the cake (picture C). Insert the candles into the middle to serve.

A

B

C

Bunny cake

This rascally rabbit is surprisingly easy to make out of two round cakes

RATING

SERVES 16

YOU WILL NEED
1 quantity Victoria sponge mixture baked in 2 x 15cm round deep tins for 45 mins (see p14), cooled

1 quantity vanilla buttercream (see p22)

1 quantity glacé icing (see p22)

TO DECORATE
Icing sugar, for dusting

250g pack ready to roll red icing by Sainsbury's

½ x 70g pack white chocolate buttons by Sainsbury's

100g desiccated coconut

60g ready to roll pink icing

20g ready to roll black icing

10 dark chocolate chips

1 strawberry lace by Sainsbury's, cut in half

YOU WILL ALSO NEED
1 large rectangular cake board

4cm-5cm round cutter

3cm round cutter

1 fine paint brush

PER SERVING
659 cals, 34.1g fat, 20.6g sat fat, 71.5g total sugars, 0.23g salt

1 To make the ears, cut equal-sized ear-shaped pieces of sponge away from the sides of one cake (see diagram, below; and picture A). The remaining sponge will form the bow tie. Remove one pointy end from each cake ear.

2 Halve each piece of cake horizontally and fill with a quarter of the buttercream. Sandwich back together on a cake board and fit the flat ends of the ears snugly to the round 'face' cake. Cover all of the cake parts with half of the remaining buttercream. Chill for 10-15 mins. Spread the remaining buttercream over the face and ears only, setting the bow tie aside.

3 Dust a surface with icing sugar and roll out the red icing to a rectangle about 20cm x 30cm x 4mm thick. Use a rolling pin to drape the icing over the bow tie. Smooth down to cover, then trim the edges of the icing (picture B). Dot the top, front and sides with the buttons, brushing with glacé icing to secure. Score 2 lines in the tie to finish.

4 Cover the face and ears with the coconut (picture C). Dust a surface with icing sugar and roll out the pink icing to 3mm thick. Use a knife to cut out 2 pointed ovals the same shape as the ears, but 1cm-2cm smaller. Use the 4cm-5cm cutter to cut out a circle for the nose. Roll the black icing to 3mm thick. Use the 3cm cutter to cut out the eyes. Brush the ears, nose and eyes with glacé icing and stick to the cake.

5 Add the chocolate chips (pointed side down) under the nose, for whiskers, and the strawberry lace as a mouth.

A

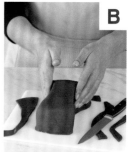
B

C

ear
bow tie
ear

Treasure chest cake

Shiver me timbers - little pirates will love this treasure trove of goodies

RATING 🧁🧁

SERVES 12

YOU WILL NEED
½ quantity chocolate sponge mixture baked in a 2lb (900g) loaf tin for 45 mins (see p16), cooled

½ quantity rich dark chocolate buttercream (see p23)

TO DECORATE
50g dark chocolate, melted (see p25)

250g pack ready to roll yellow icing by Sainsbury's

100g ready to roll chocolate flavour icing

Icing sugar, for dusting

2 tsp apricot glaze by Sainsbury's

75g digestive biscuits, finely crushed

1 tsp gold lustre

1-2 tbsp gold pearls by Sainsbury's

84g bag pirate milk chocolate coins by Sainsbury's

½ x 227g bag assorted toffees by Sainsbury's

84g pack pirate milk chocolate bars by Sainsbury's

YOU WILL ALSO NEED
25cm square gold cake board

3 cocktail sticks

PER SERVING
712 cals, 32.6g fat, 17.8g sat fat, 82.7g total sugars, 0.46g salt

1 Halve the cake horizontally and cover the top and sides of each half with the buttercream. Dip a fork in the melted dark chocolate and run the prongs along the loaf in horizontal lines to create the texture of wood (picture A). Chill slightly in the fridge.

2 Knead the yellow and chocolate icings together to an even golden brown colour. Dust a surface with icing sugar and roll out the icing to 4mm thick. Cover the cake board with the icing and trim to fit. Reserve the trimmings. Brush the covered cake board with apricot glaze, then sprinkle over the biscuit crumbs to look like sand. Set aside.

3 Roll out the icing trimmings to 5mm thick. Cut out 4 strips (roughly 1cm x 15cm each), and cut an oval from the same icing (about 3cm x 2cm) for the keyhole. Use a skewer to create a hole. On one side, brush the long icing strips with gold lustre and dot with the gold pearls at 1cm intervals (to look like nails). Brush the other side with the apricot glaze and wrap around the loaf halves, sticky side down (picture B). Brush the keyhole on one side with the glaze and stick onto the front of the chest.

4 Place the bottom half of the loaf on the cake board, then push in 3 cocktail sticks along the back of the chest Arrange the coins, toffees and gold bars on and around the loaf, then top with the other loaf half, resting down on the cocktail sticks to secure it and create a hinged effect (picture C).

Surprise cake

This cake comes with a big surprise - cut the vanilla sponge open and sweets spill out of the middle! Decorate with hundreds and thousands and an icing bow for a lovely finish

RATING

SERVES 32

YOU WILL NEED
2 quantities Victoria sponge mixture baked in 2 x 20cm round deep cake tins for 1 hour 10 mins (see p14), cooled

1 quantity vanilla buttercream (see p22)

TO DECORATE
75g pack dolly mixtures by Sainsbury's

250g pack basics midget gems

75g pack mini jelly beans by Sainsbury's

2 x 250g packs ready to roll yellow icing by Sainsbury's

3 x 80g packs multicoloured 100s & 1000s by Sainsbury's

YOU WILL ALSO NEED
400g empty and clean soup tin

25cm round silver cake board by Sainsbury's

PER SERVING
523 cals, 22.6g fat, 12.7g sat fat, 59.8g total sugars, 0.23g salt

1 Trim the tops of the cakes, if necessary (see p21), to create a flat surface. Turn both cakes upside down so the flattest surfaces are at the top. Use the clean soup tin to press down into the centre of each of the cooled cakes to make a hole (picture A). Slice one of the stamped-out circles of cake horizontally and reserve one half.

2 Sandwich the two main cakes together with a little buttercream and place on the cake board. Fill the middle with 'surprise' sweets (picture B) such as dolly mixtures, midget gems and mini jelly beans, then place the small reserved cake circle on top to make a lid.

3 Using a palette knife, spread the remaining buttercream over the top and around the outside of the cake (picture C).

TURN OVER FOR THE REMAINING RECIPE STEPS

Surprise cake (continued)

4 Roll out the icing to 2 rectangular shapes about 4mm thick and cut 4 strips of icing (about 25cm x 2cm; 2 from each rectangle).

5 Re-roll the icing trimmings and cut out a double bow shape, joined together at one end. Fold in half to form the bow (picture D), then pinch the centre together slightly. Cut another small strip of icing and wrap it around the middle of the bow (picture E). To finish, push the handle of a wooden spoon between the folded over pieces of the bow to keep them apart. Set aside until firm. See p33 for an alternative method for making icing bows.

6 Place the icing strips on the top of the cake in a cross shape to make a ribbon effect, then press lightly onto the sides of the cake, all the way to the bottom. Trim off any excess.

7 Using the flat of your hand, carefully press the 100s & 1000s all over the surface of the cake (picture F) and in between the yellow icing strips until it is completely covered on all sides.

8 Where the strips cross in the middle of the top of the cake, brush with a little water. Position the bow on top and press lightly to secure it in place.

Cook's tip: You can easily adapt this cake to make it suitable for grown-ups. Instead of filling the middle with sweets for kids, you could fill it with liqueur chocolates or even a boxed up surprise for a loved one!

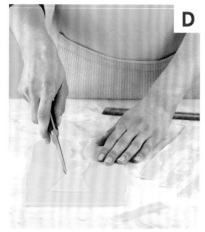

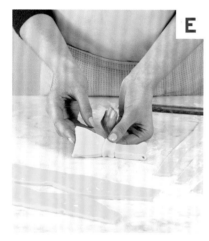

Down Mexico way

This cake is inspired by the Mexican piñata tradition where fruit and sweets are hidden inside a papier-mâché figure or piece of pottery that kids take turns to try to bash open to get the goodies! You could fill the centre with little toys (just be wary of choking hazards for small children, though).

Seaside cake

This summery seaside delight is topped with 'ice creams' made from cake and piped buttercream, and lots and lots of 'sand'!

RATING 🧁🧁🧁

SERVES 32

YOU WILL NEED
2 quantities Victoria sponge mixture; 6 tbsp of the mixture divided between 3 flat-bottomed ice cream cones and baked for 20 mins, then cooled; the remainder divided between 3 x 18cm round deep tins and baked for 50 mins (see p14), cooled

1 quantity vanilla buttercream (see p22)

4 tbsp strawberry jam

TO DECORATE
1 Cadbury Flake 99

76g pack caramel & chocolate flavoured writing icing by Sainsbury's

1 tsp coloured vermicelli by Sainsbury's

Icing sugar, for dusting

2 x 250g packs ready to roll blue icing by Sainsbury's

100g rich tea biscuits, finely crushed

100g ready to roll white icing

100g ready to roll red icing

100g ready to roll yellow icing

125g ready to roll green icing

50g ready to roll chocolate icing (optional)

100g ready to roll fuchsia pink icing (optional)

YOU WILL ALSO NEED
1 disposable piping bag

1 star-shaped piping nozzle

1 large round cake plate

Cocktail sticks

1 drinking straw

PER SERVING
551 cals, 24.5g fat, 13.6g sat fat, 64.4g total sugars, 0.25g salt

1 Trim the tops of the cakes that have been baked in the cones (see p21) to create a flat surface. Fit the piping bag with the star-shaped nozzle and spoon a quarter of the buttercream into the bag. Pipe the buttercream onto the top of the cakes in the cones to create an ice-cream effect (picture A). Decorate with the flake, writing icing and coloured vermicelli strands.

2 Trim the tops of the sponge cakes to create flat surfaces (see p21), then sandwich them together with thin layers of buttercream and jam. Put the cake on a wire rack, then spread the remaining buttercream over the top and sides of the cake stack to cover completely (picture B).

3 Dust a surface with icing sugar and roll each pack of blue icing out to a rectangle, each measuring about 30cm x 10cm x 4mm thick. Using a cocktail stick, score a wave shape onto the long side of each piece. When you're happy

 A
 B
 C

TURN OVER FOR THE REMAINING RECIPE STEPS ▶

Seaside cake (continued)

with the shape, cut it out using a sharp knife (picture C). Press the waves around the base of the cake, making sure the seams join at the sides of the cake (trim to fit as necessary) – the buttercream will help the waves to stick in place on the cake.

4 Scatter and press the crushed biscuits over the rest of the cake to create a sand effect (picture D). You will need to gather the 'sand' several times from under the wire rack and re-apply until it completely covers the cake. Carefully transfer the cake to the cake plate.

5 To make the napkin for the top of the cake, roll out 50g white icing to a 2mm thick x 12cm square. Create detail around the edges of the napkin by pressing with a cocktail stick. Lift the edges with a fork or a small spoon to give the effect of a fluttering napkin, then position on top of the cake.

6 Knead the red icing with half of the yellow icing to create a deep orange colour. Knead together until the colours are fully combined.

7 Use the orange icing and the remaining ready to roll icings (yellow, green, chocolate and pink) to make seaweed and sea creatures. For the seaweed, roll green icing to 1mm-2mm thick and cut out wavy lengths. The seaweed can be used to cover the seams on the blue icing. For the fish, roll small pieces of icing into oval shapes, attach tail-shaped pieces of icing with a little water and score on details with a cocktail stick. If you like, add fins or stripes in different-coloured icing. For the octopus, roll a small piece of green icing into a ball, create eyes with pieces of white icing and pupils with writing icing pen. Make the legs with more green icing and create markings on them using the end of a straw. Stick on the legs with a little water. For the starfish, roll out the pink icing to 5mm-6mm thick, then stamp out starfish with a star-shaped cutter. Use writing icing pens for detail. For the pebbles, marble a little brown and white icing together, roll into small balls and flatten. For the coral, roll out the yellow icing to 1mm-2mm thick, cut into short strips and join the ends with a little water to form hoops. Pipe a small amount of the writing icing onto the back of seaweed and ocean creatures, leave them for 2 mins (this makes the surface stickier), then attach to the cake (picture E).

8 To finish, insert 3 cocktail sticks into the 'napkin', then push an ice-cream cone cake onto each cocktail stick to secure it in place (picture F).

D

E

F

Cook's tip

If you don't have 3 x 18cm round deep tins to bake the Victoria sponges in, you could make 2 slightly deeper cakes in 2 x 18cm tins instead. When lining the tins, make sure the baking paper comes at least 2cm above the top of the tins to allow for the rising of the cakes. Cook the cakes for 1 hour-1 hour 15 mins.

Dragon cake

You'll wow everyone with this fantastic creation – a fabulous dragon

RATING

SERVES 40

YOU WILL NEED
2 quantities vanilla buttercream (see p22), mixed with 6 tsp green food colouring and 2 tsp black food colouring

1 quantity Victoria sponge mixture baked in 2 x 15cm round cake tins for 30 mins (see p14), cooled

1 quantity Victoria sponge mixture baked in a 32cm x 22cm x 5cm deep rectangular baking tray for 1 hour (see p14), cooled

TO DECORATE
200g ready to roll green icing

Icing sugar, for dusting

100g ready to roll orange icing

1 white chocolate button, halved

Dark chocolate writing icing pen (from 76g pack caramel & chocolate writing icing by Sainsbury's)

1 liquorice pin wheel

150g caster sugar

YOU WILL ALSO NEED
1 large rectangular cake board

4 round cutters: 5cm, 6cm, 7cm and 8cm

1 long wooden skewer

1 fine paint brush

1 disposable piping bag

1 large round piping nozzle

PER SERVING
457 cals, 23g fat, 13.1g sat fat, 49.5g total sugars, 0.18g salt

1 Trim the tops of the cakes, if necessary (see p21), to create a flat surface. Use a little of the dark green vanilla buttercream to sandwich together the 2 round cakes, then transfer to the cake board.

2 Position the head (1) and tail (5) templates (see p188-189) and 4 x round cutters on the rectangular sponge (picture A) and cut out the shapes. Cut the 6cm round sponge in half to make 2 small semi-circles. This will give you 3 small round sponges, 1 tail sponge, 1 oval sponge and 2 semi-circle sponges.

3 Spread the bottom of each small sponge round with buttercream and position, starting with the largest round, in size order one on top of the other on one side of the main round cake. Insert the skewer to secure the rounds in place (cutting to the right length). Top with the oval shape, then make two small cuts in the oval sponge to create a mouth.

4 With a sharp knife, trim the main cake to a rounded, ball-like shape.

A

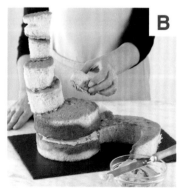

B

C

TURN OVER FOR THE REMAINING RECIPE STEPS ▶

Dragon cake (continued)

5 Position the tail next to the main cake. Place one sponge semi-circle on top of the main cake and the other at the thick part of the tail (picture B). Secure with a little buttercream.

6 Coat the whole cake in a thin layer of green buttercream using a small palette knife.

7 For the head detail, knead the green icing, then use 20g to roll into a small squashed oval shape, 5g to roll into a small sausage shape, then roll two pea-sized balls. Position on the top of the oval sponge to create the contours of the head and nostrils (picture C).

8 Reserving 40g for the eyes, feet and arms, roll out the remaining green icing to 3mm thick and cut out an 18cm circle using template 4 on p188-189. Use this to cover the head (picture D), pressing into the buttercream to attach. Trim the excess icing around the neck with a sharp knife. Reserve the trimmings. Using the end of the paint brush, make 2 indentations in the snout for nostrils.

9 For the dragon's belly, dust a surface with icing sugar and roll out half the orange icing to 3mm thick. Cut out an oval about 11cm x 5cm. Press this onto the buttercream. Use a palette knife to make indentations across the oval to create lines in the belly (picture E).

10 Put most of the remaining buttercream in a piping bag fitted with a large round nozzle. Working from the top of the neck in vertical lines, create scales by piping on blobs of buttercream, dragging down slightly as you pull away (picture F). Continue along the top of the tail; for the sides of the tail, spread a layer of leftover buttercream with a palette knife.

11 For the eyes, roll 2 x 5g balls from the reserved green icing, flatten slightly and press half a chocolate button into each one. Fix to the head with a little water. Once in place, dot with a little of the dark chocolate writing icing for the pupils. Cut 5cm from the liquorice, snip the end with scissors and press into the mouth to make the tongue.

12 Roll out the remaining orange icing to 3mm thick and cut out 2 triangular shapes for the wings and 1 triangular shape for the tail using templates 2 and 3 on p188. Using a sharp knife, cut out a 13cm x 2.5cm strip, then cut zig-zags into the strip along one long edge to make a collar. Press these pieces onto the dragon.

13 For the feet, slightly squash 2 x 10g balls of reserved green icing and cut out small triangles to create toes. For the arms, roll 2 x 5g sausage-shapes from the reserved green icing, making one end slightly thicker than the other. As before, cut out small triangles at the larger end to create finger shapes. Snip off small pieces of liquorice and press onto the fingers and toes for claws (use writing icing to help stick, if needed). Position the feet on the board at the front of the dragon and stick the arms on the body.

14 To make the caramel shards for the tail spikes, line a baking tray with baking paper. Heat the caster sugar in a small pan over a low heat. Shake the pan a little until the sugar starts to clump together. When it has fully melted and turned a golden colour, pour onto the paper and set aside to cool. Once cold and hard, break into shards, and press along the dragon's tail and back (picture G).

D

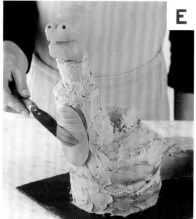

E

F

G

Fairy tale castle cake

Kids will be enchanted by our fairy tale cake complete with Rapunzel in the tower!

RATING

SERVES 30

YOU WILL NEED
1 quantity Victoria sponge mixture baked in 2 x 15cm round cake tins for 45 mins (see p14), cooled

2 quantities vanilla buttercream (see p22)

TO DECORATE
2 x 365g packs jumbo strawberry & vanilla Swiss roll by Sainsbury's

2 tbsp pink food colouring, plus a few extra drops

2 tbsp strawberry jam

250g icing sugar, plus extra for dusting

5 x 250g packs ready to roll pink icing by Sainsbury's

2 x 190g packs raspberry Swiss rolls by Sainsbury's

5g ready to roll black icing

100g ready to roll white icing

10g mini marshmallows

10g ready to roll yellow icing

A few drops of green food colouring

1 pack mini blossom cake decorations by Sainsbury's

4 ice cream cones

2 tbsp apricot glaze by Sainsbury's, warmed

½ x 75g pot pink glimmer sugar by Sainsbury's

70g pack white chocolate buttons by Sainsbury's, halved

YOU WILL ALSO NEED
1 large round cake board

6 long skewers

Cocktail stick

2 disposable icing bags

1 small round writing piping nozzle

1 large round piping nozzle

PER SERVING
791 cals, 29.6g fat, 17.5g sat fat, 110.2g total sugars, 0.35g salt

1 Assemble the elements for this cake on your work surface so you're ready to start (picture A). Cut the jumbo Swiss rolls to 19cm in length.

2 Mix the 2 tbsp pink food colouring into the buttercream. Trim the 2 x 15cm cakes, then sandwich them together with a little of the buttercream and the jam. Put the cake on the cake board. Spread the buttercream up the sides and over the top of the cake, this is your 'crumb' layer. Chill for 10 mins, then repeat with another layer of buttercream and set the remaining buttercream aside.

3 Dust a surface with icing sugar. Knead the pink icing packs together, then divide into 4 even quantities and roll each out to a rough rectangle about 4mm thick. Cut out 2 x 23cm x 16cm rectangles and place on baking paper that has been cut slightly larger than the icing rectangle. Lay each icing rectangle so the shortest end is facing towards you, then spread with a thin layer of the reserved buttercream. Place one of the small Swiss rolls

A

B

C

TURN OVER FOR THE REMAINING RECIPE STEPS ▶

Fairy tale castle cake (continued)

at the short end and use the paper paper to help roll it around the Swiss roll (picture B). Fold the ends of the icing over the top of the Swiss rolls. Repeat with the remaining small Swiss roll. Set aside.

4 Cut out 2 x 25cm x 21cm rectangles from the remaining icing pieces. Repeat the previous step to cover the larger Swiss rolls with the pink icing. Set aside.

5 Push a skewer into the side of the cake (2cm from the base) so that it comes out on the opposite side, then repeat with 2 more skewers, spacing them approximately 2cm above each other. Repeat across the opposite side of the cake. Push the Swiss rolls onto the skewers to make the towers of the castle, with the small towers at the front and the larger ones at the back (picture C).

6 Place the icing sugar in a bowl and mix in 3 tbsp water until you have a smooth glacé icing that coats the back of a spoon.

7 Roll a small piece of the black icing into a ball to make a door handle, then roll out 50g white icing into a rectangle 3mm thick and cut out 4 window shutters and a door with a sharp knife. Press the door and marshmallows into position on the main cake - they will stick to the buttercream. Use a little of the glacé icing to stick the shutters onto the towers. Marble 15g white icing with a little piece of the black to make 'stones' (picture D) and set aside.

8 To make 'Rapunzel's' face, mix a little yellow and white icing together (you will need about 5g icing in total) with a drop of pink food colouring and roll into a ball. Attach to a small oval shape of white icing. For the hair, roll 5g yellow icing so you have a long thin sausage shape; flatten at one end and score in lines with a knife. Use the glacé icing to attach to the cake. Make simple features with a cocktail stick.

9 Stir the green food colouring into the remaining glacé icing. Fill an icing bag fitted with a small round writing nozzle and pipe vines and grass onto the cake (picture E). Stick on 16 mini blossom decorations and scatter the 'stones' around the base.

10 Fill an icing bag fitted with a large round nozzle with the remaining pink buttercream. Using a circular motion, cover the exposed cake on top of the towers.

11 Brush the sides of the ice cream cones with the warmed apricot glaze, then hold them over a bowl and sprinkle with the glimmer sugar (picture F). Put the cones on top of the buttercream to create turrets. Secure the remaining mini blossom decorations around the turrets using a little apricot glaze.

12 Push the white chocolate button halves into the buttercream at the base of the turrets. Finally, use 10g white icing to make four balls and use a little apricot glaze to fix them to the top of the turrets.

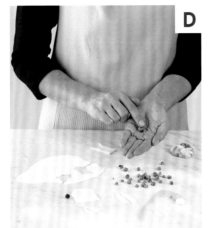

D

E

F

Let down your hair!
The story of Rapunzel has enraptured little readers since it was first published by the Brothers Grimm in 1812. The story of the girl with the long golden tresses kept in a high tower by a wicked witch follows the familiar route of love and finally rescue – after many suitably dire travails – by a handsome prince!

Choo-choo train cake

Stand back and take the applause when you bring this beautiful cake to the table

RATING

SERVES 24

YOU WILL NEED
1 ½ quantities chocolate sponge mixture baked in a 32cm x 22cm x 5cm deep rectangular baking tray for 1 hour 15 mins (see p16), cooled

½ quantity rich white chocolate buttercream (see p23)

1 quantity glacé icing (see p22)

½ quantity biscuit dough mixture (see p19)

TO DECORATE
Icing sugar, for dusting

3 x 250g packs ready to roll green icing by Sainsbury's, kneaded together

½ x 167g pack chocolate crunchy mint sticks by Sainsbury's, half halved; the rest left whole

½ x 400g ginger loaf cake by Sainsbury's

250g ready to roll chocolate flavour icing

2 tbsp apricot glaze by Sainsbury's, warmed

95g pack basics chocolate flavoured Swiss roll sponge, cut to a 6cm-long piece

1 Tunnocks tea cake

4 white chocolate buttons

8 Sainsbury's Bakery milk chocolate mini rolls, 3 rolls cut into 3 pieces; the rest left whole

1 mini chocolate wafer roll by Sainsbury's

2 chocolate bourbon creams by Sainsbury's

¼ tsp edible gold lustre by Sainsbury's

3 x 6cm Cadbury Flake 99s

8 mini blossom cake decorations by Sainsbury's

YOU WILL ALSO NEED
1 rectangular cake board

1 fine paint brush

Tree-shaped cutters

PER SERVING
830 cals, 35.8g fat, 19.6g sat fat, 94.4g total sugars, 0.48g salt

1 Put the cake on the cake board and spread the top and sides with the buttercream (picture A).

2 Dust a surface with icing sugar and roll out the green icing to 4mm thick. Use a rolling pin to drape the icing over the cake. Smooth down to cover the cake, then trim the edges of the icing, reserving the trimmings.

3 Brush glacé icing onto the back of the mint sticks and stick onto the cake to make a train track, using the full sticks to make the track lines and the halves to make the railway sleepers (picture B).

4 From the ginger loaf, cut a 5cm x 4cm x 6cm piece for the back cabin of the locomotive and a 7cm x 4cm x 4cm x 4cm cart shape for the trailer (picture C). Dust a surface with icing sugar. Roll out the chocolate icing to 1cm-2mm thick. Brush each of the ginger loaf pieces with the warmed apricot glaze, then cover completely with the chocolate icing and set aside. Brush the 6cm Swiss roll with the glaze

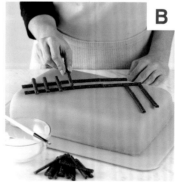

TURN OVER FOR THE REMAINING RECIPE STEPS ▶

Choo-choo train cake (continued)

and also cover with the chocolate icing, leaving the ends uncovered.

5 Complete the locomotive: with the glacé icing, stick the tea cake onto the front of the Swiss roll piece. Put more glacé icing on the back of the Swiss roll piece and stick the cabin onto it. Stick 2 white buttons onto either side to create windows. Finish the cabin with the wheels: put a little glacé icing where you will stick the wheels, then place the chocolate mini roll end pieces onto the sides and hold for 1 min or so until the icing has set. Attach the other wheels of the locomotive in the same way. Use glacé icing to fix a whole chocolate mini roll and the mini wafer roll on top as chimneys. Gently lift the locomotive and place it on the tracks at the front of the cake.

6 Make the first carriage: break up the bourbon cream biscuit into small pieces and stick onto the top of the trailer with the glacé icing (picture D). Using glacé icing, stick the chocolate iced trailer onto the 2 whole mini rolls to give it wheels. Sprinkle with the gold lustre and place the completed trailer on the tracks, behind the locomotive.

7 For the final log carriage: split the last remaining bourbon cream and scrape off and discard the filling so you have 2 single planks. Top the clean sides with the flake 'logs', securing them together with glacé icing. Place the final 2 mini rolls onto the remaining part of the tracks, then sit the log carriage on top.

8 Arrange the mini blossom cake decorations on the green icing, fixing in place with glacé icing.

9 Roll out the biscuit base dough to 3mm thick. Stamp out 3 tree shapes with different-sized cutters (picture D), and use a knife to cut out 3 triangle shapes to make supports. Bake in the oven at 190°C, fan 170°C, gas 5 for 10-12 mins. Set aside to cool on a wire rack. Roll out the green icing trimmings to 2mm thick. Stamp out trees with the cutters and attach them to the biscuits with the glacé icing (picture E). Use a little glacé icing to attach the supporting triangles to the backs of the trees and position them on the cake or, if you like, leave the triangles off one or two of the biscuits and press the trees to the front of the cake instead.

Cook's tip

You will probably have some biscuit dough trimmings left over after stamping out the trees. Don't waste them – both the raw dough and cooked biscuits freeze well, so either roll up the dough and pop it in a piece of cling film in the freezer or cut it into shapes and bake at the same time as the trees.

Rocket cake

Blast off to the stars with this out-of-this-world cake creation

RATING

SERVES 16

YOU WILL NEED
1 quantity chocolate sponge mixture baked in 32cm x 22cm x 5cm deep rectangular baking tray for 1 hour (see p16), cooled

1 quantity rich white chocolate buttercream (see p23)

TO DECORATE
2 tsp blue food colouring

Icing sugar, for dusting

2 x 250g packs ready to roll red icing by Sainsbury's, kneaded together

50g strawberry pencils by Sainsbury's

2 strawberry laces by Sainsbury's

1/2 x 83g pot party sprinkles by Sainsbury's (you will need 20g 100s & 1000s; 10g chocolate beans; and 10g sugar stars from the pack)

2 tbsp apricot glaze by Sainsbury's, warmed

3 ice cream cones, tops separated from the ends

3 tbsp blue glimmer sugar by Sainsbury's

50g ready to roll yellow icing

YOU WILL ALSO NEED
1 large dark rectangular cake board

1 small star-shaped cutter

4cm round cutter

Small number cutters

PER SERVING
814 cals, 36.4g fat, 19.6g sat fat, 99.2g total sugars, 0.4g salt

1 Trim the top of the cake, if necessary (see p21), and place, flattest side up, on a cutting board. Using the triangle template on p189, cut 2 triangles from one end for the rocket fins. Cut 2 x 2cm strips from the longer sides to give a narrower shape. Cut a 14cm-long piece from one of the strips, slightly angling the cuts to make the base of the rocket (picture A). The remaining strips can be eaten as cook's treats! Position the fins at the base, then trim 2cm from their outer edges (picture B).

2 Gently fold the blue food colouring into the buttercream to achieve an even light blue colour (picture C). Cover the main cake with a thin layer of blue buttercream and transfer to the fridge to chill for 30 mins. Meanwhile, cover the 2 fins and the base with a thin layer of blue buttercream.

3 Dust a surface with icing sugar, then roll out the red icing to 3mm thick. Use this to cover the fins and base, trimming to fit and reserving the trimmings. Press the handle of a spatula or other kitchen utensil into the red icing to create indentations (picture D).

4 Cover the main cake in a second layer of blue buttercream. Roll out the red icing trimmings to 20cm x 24cm x 3mm thick. Use a plate to cut out a curve along one of the longer sides (picture E) and use this to cover the nose of the rocket. Trim any excess icing from the base of the cake and reserve the trimmings. Cut a 5cm piece of strawberry pencil and push it into the nose of the rocket. Transfer the body of the rocket to your dark rectangular cake board.

A

B

C

Rocket cake (continued)

5 Cut the remaining strawberry pencils into 2cm lengths and arrange about 1cm from the bottom of the rocket in a slight curve. Cover the area below with 100s & 1000s, brushing away any that fall onto the board with a pastry brush. Position the remaining strawberry pencil pieces in a curve at the top of the cake on the red icing, using a little water to stick them down, if needed. Gently press a line of yellow chocolate beans into the buttercream below the curve.

6 Position the fins next to the body of the rocket and the base at the bottom. Use a little water to stick them on.

7 Brush the ice cream cone tops with apricot glaze. Holding them over a bowl, use a teaspoon to coat them in the glimmer sugar (picture F). Gently push the narrower ends of the cone tops into the base of the rocket.

8 Roll out the yellow icing to 2mm thick and cut out 10 stars. Use 6 to decorate the sides of the rocket and the remainder to decorate the board. Cut strawberry laces to fit in two lines down the length of the rocket, then press down gently about 5cm in from the edges. Use a 4cm round cutter to stamp out a disc. Use the number cutters to stamp out the age of the birthday boy or girl from the leftover red icing and position on top of the disc on the cake, using a little water to stick them down. Scatter the sugar stars on the board to decorate.

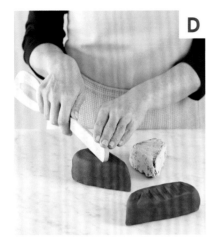

D

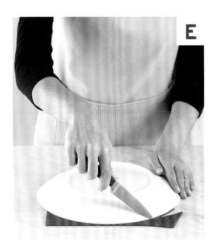

E

F

Ready for launch!

Personalise the cake by cutting out more yellow ready to roll icing rounds, then using letter cutters, cut out the letters needed for the birthday child's name. If you don't have letter cutters, use a sharp knife and cut out by hand. The name can be spelt vertically going down the rocket body – or across if the name is very short.

Football shirt cake

You'll shoot to the top of the league with this winning football shirt cake. To score with the home crowd, choose the colours of their favourite team

RATING 🧁

SERVES 24

YOU WILL NEED
1½ quantities chocolate sponge cake mixture baked in a 22cm x 32cm x 5cm deep baking tray for 1 hour 15 mins (see p16), cooled

½ quantity vanilla buttercream (see p22)

2 tbsp glacé icing (see p22)

TO DECORATE
Icing sugar, for dusting

4 x 250g packs ready to roll yellow icing, kneaded together

150g ready to roll green icing

50g ready to roll blue icing

1 pack 12 football cake decorations by Sainsbury's

YOU WILL ALSO NEED
1 large rectangular cake board

Alphabet cutters

PER SERVING
664 cals, 26.2g fat, 14.8g sat fat, 82.9g total sugars, 0.38g salt

1 Level the top of the cake with a serrated knife (see p21). Halve the cake horizontally, spread one cut side with half of the buttercream and sandwich back together.

2 Cut a 4cm x 20cm strip from one side of the cake (see diagram, below). Cut 2 small rectangles from the strip of cake and attach to the sides of the cake with some of the buttercream. Trim to give the sleeves a T-shirt shape (picture A). Spread the rest of the buttercream over the top and sides of the cake, then put it on the cake board.

3 Dust a surface with icing sugar and roll out the yellow icing to a rectangle about 35cm x 42cm. Use a rolling pin to drape the icing over the cake; smooth down to cover. You will need to cut the icing around both sleeves (picture B), which will leave 2 small square areas of cake un-iced. Trim the excess icing from the base of the cake. Re-roll the trimmings and cut out 2 squares to fill the un-iced areas, smoothing over the joins with your fingertips.

4 Roll out the green icing to 3mm thick and cut out 2 x 2.5cm x 20cm strips and 2 x 5cm x 10cm diamond shapes to fit the sides and sleeves of the shirt.

5 Roll out the blue icing to 3mm thick. With a knife, cut out a number and use alphabet cutters to stamp out the letters of a name. Attach to the shirt with glacé icing (picture C). Decorate the cake sides with the football cake decorations, attached with dots of glacé icing.

A

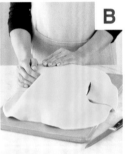

B

C

Butterfly cake

The perfect choice for any little nature lover's birthday party

RATING

SERVES 16

YOU WILL NEED
1½ quantities Victoria sponge mixture baked in 32cm x 22cm x 5cm deep rectangular baking tray for 1 hour 15 mins (see p14), cooled

1 quantity rich white chocolate buttercream (see p23)

TO DECORATE
500g pack ready to roll white icing by Sainsbury's

250g pack ready to roll pink icing by Sainsbury's

Icing sugar, for dusting

2 tsp apricot glaze by Sainsbury's

½ pack mini blossom cake decorations by Sainsbury's

4 tbsp strawberry jam

3 x 38g packs Smarties

4 tbsp white shimmer pearls by Sainsbury's

2 tbsp blue glimmer sugar by Sainsbury's

2 tbsp gold glimmer sugar by Sainsbury's

2 tbsp pink glimmer sugar by Sainsbury's

1 strawberry lace by Sainsbury's

YOU WILL ALSO NEED
1 rectangular cake board

1 disposable piping bag

1 large star-shaped piping nozzle

PER SERVING
602 cals, 31.7g fat, 18.2g sat fat, 61.4g total sugars, 0.26g salt

1 Knead the white and pink icings together until well combined and smooth. Dust a surface with icing sugar and roll out the icing to 3mm thick. Lightly brush the cake board with apricot glaze, then cover with the icing and trim to fit. Brush the backs of the blossom decorations with the apricot glaze and stick onto the iced board around the edge. Set aside.

2 On a cutting board, cut the cake into shape using the template on p188 (picture A). Cut in half horizontally, spread with jam and a quarter of the buttercream and sandwich together.

3 Cover the top and sides with a thin layer of buttercream. Chill for 30 mins before spreading over another layer of buttercream (about half of the remaining buttercream), reserving the rest for piping. Carefully transfer the cake to the icing-covered cake board.

4 Spoon the reserved buttercream into a piping bag with a star-shaped piping nozzle. Pipe large stars down the centre of the body, then smaller ones around the outline of the wings and across the centre, separating the top and bottom wings with blobs (picture B). Arrange Smarties on the smaller stars only (picture C).

5 Split the wings again down the middle using the shimmer pearls. Make a double line of pearls diagonally across each wing. In the top half of the upper wings, spoon the blue glimmer sugar over both sides. Then use the gold glimmer sugar over the bottom half.

6 For the bottom wings, use pink glimmer sugar on the top half, and gold on the bottom half. Cut the strawberry lace in half and shape to look like butterfly antennae on your cake board.

Chimp chocolate cake

This cheeky chocolate cake is simple to make and decorate for a children's birthday party

RATING

SERVES 24

YOU WILL NEED
1 quantity chocolate sponge mixture baked in 2 x 23cm round tins for 40-45 mins (see p16), cooled

1 quantity vanilla buttercream (see p22)

TO DECORATE
Icing sugar, for dusting

750g ready to roll chocolate flavour icing

150g ready to roll ivory icing

YOU WILL ALSO NEED
1 large round cake board

4 cocktail sticks

PER SERVING
543 cals, 24.5g fat, 14.1g sat fat, 65.7g total sugars, 0.28g salt

1 If necessary, trim the tops of the cakes to make them level (see p21). Sandwich them together using one-third of the buttercream, then put the cake on the cake board. Spread the remaining buttercream over the top and sides of the cake.

2 Dust a surface with icing sugar and roll out the chocolate icing to a large 3mm-thick circle. Use a rolling pin to drape the icing over the cake, then smooth down to cover the cake completely. Trim the edges and use the remaining icing to shape 2 ears, about 7cm x 5cm, 2 eyeballs and 2 eyebrows. Roll the remaining chocolate icing out to 5mm thick, then, by hand, cut shapes to make a smiley mouth and nostrils. Set aside.

3 Dust a surface with icing sugar and roll out the ivory icing to 5mm thick. Using the template on p191, cut out the shape for the chimp's face from the icing (picture A), then cut out 2 shapes to go inside the ears and roll 2 small balls for the pupils.

4 Brush the chimp's face with a little cooled boiled water, then stick the face onto the cake, gently pressing down with the palm of your hand to secure.

5 Brush the backs of the eyes, eyebrows, nostrils, mouth shapes and pupils with water, then stick them to the face (picture B).

6 Brush the ears with water, and stick the ivory inner ears into place. Secure the ears to the cake using cocktail sticks (picture C).

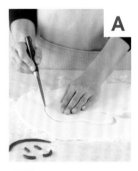

A

B

C

Sheep cake

No need to be sheepish if you can turn out this fun-filled animal cake. He's easy to make and will be the star attraction of any kids' party

RATING

SERVES 24

YOU WILL NEED
1 quantity Victoria sponge mixture baked in 2 x 23cm round cake tins for 35-40 mins (see p14), cooled

1 quantity rich white chocolate buttercream (see p23)

½ quantity royal icing (see p24)

TO DECORATE
Icing sugar, for dusting

1kg pack ready to roll white icing by Sainsbury's

250g pack ready to roll black icing by Sainsbury's

2 x 180g packs white mini marshmallows by Sainsbury's

YOU WILL ALSO NEED
1 large round cake board

4 cocktail sticks

PER SERVING
665 cals, 23.2g fat, 14.4g sat fat, 99g total sugars, 0.18g salt

1 If necessary, trim the tops of the cakes to make them level (see p21). Sandwich them together using one-third of the buttercream and put the cake on the cake board. Spread the remaining buttercream over the top and sides of the cake.

2 Dust a surface with icing sugar and roll out the white icing to 4mm thick. Use a rolling pin to drape the icing over the cake, then smooth down all over to create an even surface. Trim the edges, reserving the trimmings. Roll out two small balls from the remaining white icing for the eyeballs and set aside.

3 Roll out the black icing to 3mm thick and cut out a 12cm x 19cm oval. From the remaining black icing, roll 2 small balls for the pupils and stick them on the white eyeballs. Roll 2 balls (60g each) from the remaining icing for the feet and set aside. Mould 2 ears out of the remaining icing, pushing your thumb into the icing to create an ear cavity.

4 Brush the oval face with water on one side and stick into the centre of the cake. Attach the eyes to the face, using a little water to help them stick, then use the rounded end of a knife to create the nose and mouth in the black icing (picture A). Use cocktail sticks to attach the ears (picture B). Mould the feet into balls, then squash into a cylinder shape and attach to the base of the cake with cocktail sticks.

5 Brush the royal icing onto a small section on the top of the cake (picture C) and stick on some marshmallows. Continue, working in small sections so the icing doesn't set, until completely covered.

A

B

C

Little piggy cake

This little pig is quick and very straightforward to decorate. With her glittery cheeks and cute rosette, she'll bring a smile to any child's face

RATING 🧁

SERVES 24

YOU WILL NEED
1 quantity chocolate sponge mixture baked in 2 x 23cm round cake tins for 40-45 mins (see p16), cooled

1 quantity strawberry buttercream (see p23)

1 quantity glacé icing (see p22)

TO DECORATE
Icing sugar, to dust

4 x 250g packs ready to roll pink icing by Sainsbury's

70g pack rainbow buttons by Sainsbury's

4 white marshmallows, cut in half

2 blue and 3 red chocolate beans by Sainsbury's

2 tbsp pink glimmer sugar by Sainsbury's

1 strawberry lace

YOU WILL ALSO NEED
1 large round cake board

1 fine paint brush

9cm round cutter

6cm round cutter

PER SERVING
602 cals, 24.2g fat, 14.2g sat fat, 82.1g total sugars, 0.27g salt

1 Sandwich the cakes together with an even layer of the buttercream, then spread the rest over the top and sides of the layered cakes.

2 Dust a surface with icing sugar. Knead three packs of the pink icing together, then roll out to 4mm thick. Use a rolling pin to drape the icing over the cake, then smooth down to cover the cake completely. Trim the edges of the icing, reserving the trimmings.

3 Put the cake on the board, then stick the rainbow buttons around the base of the cake using a little of the glacé icing (picture A).

4 Make the nose: dust a surface with icing sugar and roll out the final pack of pink icing to 5mm thick. Stamp out a 9cm circle with the cutter, then use your hands to shape into an oval. Secure in place on the cake with a little of the glacé icing and create nostrils using a skewer.

5 Roll out the icing trimmings to about 5mm thick and cut 2 x 6cm circles. Shape into ovals for ears and stick on with glacé icing. Have half the ear hanging over the edge and down the side of the cake.

6 Stick 2 marshmallow halves onto the cake for eyes. Brush the remaining halves with glacé icing and make a rosette by one of the ears, sticking the red chocolate beans in the centre. Sprinkle with pink glitter. Stick the blue beans onto the eyes. Brush a little glacé icing onto the cheeks and sprinkle with pink glitter.

7 Complete the face by cutting the strawberry lace and sticking it on with a little of the glacé icing in the shape of a smiling mouth.

A

B

C

Kitty cat cake

Who can resist our deliciously lovable cat? He's an easy to make variation of the previous animal cakes and the perfect surprise for a feline-loving child

RATING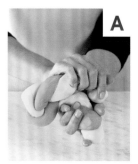

SERVES 24

YOU WILL NEED
1 quantity Victoria sponge mixture baked in 2 x 23cm round cake tins for 35-40 mins (see p14), cooled

1 quantity vanilla buttercream (see p22)

1 quantity glacé icing (see p22)

TO DECORATE
2 x 250g packs ready to roll orange icing by Sainsbury's

2 x 250g packs ready to roll yellow icing by Sainsbury's

Icing sugar, for dusting

100g ready to roll white icing

5g ready to roll green icing (or 5g of your white icing dyed with green food colouring)

20g ready to roll pink icing, rolled into a ball

3 chocolate crunchy mint sticks by Sainsbury's, halved

Black writing icing pen (from 76g pack colour writing icing pens by Sainsbury's)

2 tbsp gold pearls by Sainsbury's

YOU WILL ALSO NEED
1 large cake plate

6cm round cutter

3cm round cutter

1 fine paint brush

PER SERVING
558 cals, 22.6g fat, 14.1g sat fat, 78.2g total sugars, 0.15g salt

1 Trim the tops of the cakes if necessary (see p21), then sandwich together using one-third of the buttercream. Put the cake on a cake plate and spread the remaining buttercream over the top and sides.

2 Twist the 4 packs of orange and yellow icing together (picture A), then knead a little for a marbled effect. Dust a surface with icing sugar and roll out to 4mm thick. Use a rolling pin to drape the icing over the cake, then smooth down all over to make an even surface. Trim the edges, then use the trimmings to mould 2 ears; attach them using glacé icing.

3 Roll out the white icing to 3mm thick and cut a 1cm-wide strip to fit around the base of the cake for the collar. Stamp out the cheeks with the 6cm cutter, and the eyes and name tag with a 3cm cutter. Use a knife to cut shapes for the inner ears and the cat's stripes.

4 Brush the inside of the ears with glacé icing and stick the inner ears in place. Roll the green icing into circles and stick onto the eyes with the glacé icing. Brush the pink icing ball (for the nose), the eyes and cheeks with the glacé icing, then stick them all in place (picture B).

5 Stick the mint sticks onto the cheeks . Use writing icing to pipe a mouth (picture C) and write a name on the tag.

6 Brush the white icing stripes with glacé icing and stick on the sides and top of the cake. Brush the back of the collar with glacé icing, then fit it in place. Stick on the gold pearls and attach the name tag.

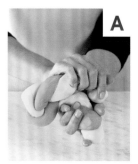

A

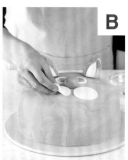

B

C

Teddy bears' picnic cake

Ah, isn't he just the sweetest? Our friendly teddy bear comes with bow tie and hat to set off his super-cute features. Another easily achievable cake that kids will fall in love with

RATING 🧁

SERVES 24

YOU WILL NEED
1 quantity chocolate sponge mixture baked in 2 x 23cm round cake tins for 45 mins (see p16), cooled

½ quantity rich chocolate buttercream (see p23)

1 quantity glacé icing (see p22)

TO DECORATE
500g pack ready to roll chocolate flavour icing by Sainsbury's

500g pack ready to roll white icing by Sainsbury's

Icing sugar, for dusting

30g ready to roll black icing

70g pack milk chocolate buttons by Sainsbury's

YOU WILL ALSO NEED
1 large round cake board

6cm round cutter

9cm round cutter

1 cocktail stick

1 fine paint brush

PER SERVING
528 cals, 22g fat, 11.5g sat fat, 68.4g total sugars, 0.27g salt

1 Trim the tops of the cakes, if necessary (see p21) to make level tops, then sandwich them together using one-third of the buttercream. Transfer the cake to the cake board and spread the remaining buttercream over the top and sides.

2 Knead 350g of the chocolate icing together with 150g of the white icing until you get a smooth mid-brown colour (picture A). This will be used for the main part of the head, the ears and the forelock.

3 Knead 50g of the chocolate icing together with 180g of the white icing until you get a smooth, even light-brown colour. This will be used for the inner ears, snout and part of the eyes.

4 Dust a surface with icing sugar and roll out the mid-brown icing to 4mm thick. Use a rolling pin to drape the icing over the cake, then smooth it down all over with the palms of your hands to get an even surface. Trim the icing at the base of the cake, reserving the trimmings.

5 Roll out the mid-brown icing trimmings to 3mm thick and cut out 2 x 6cm discs. Mould into oval shapes for the ears and set aside. With the remaining mid-brown icing, roll out a thin cigar shape, cut into 3 pieces, then bend them slightly to make a curly forelock of hair. To make the hat, roll some of the black icing into a cigar shape about 4-5cm long (picture B) and the rest into a rough circle with a flat edge. Using glacé icing, stick the two together, then attach the hair and the hat to the cake using more glacé icing.

A

B

C

Teddy bears' picnic cake (continued)

6 For the snout, dust a surface with a little more icing sugar and roll out the light-brown icing to 1cm thick. Using a 9cm round cutter, cut out a circle then, using your hands, shape it into an oval (picture C). Using the back of a knife, draw indentations for the nose and mouth, then create hair follicles with a cocktail stick (picture D). Stick it onto the middle of the cake with a little of the glacé icing.

7 Using the light-brown icing trimmings, roll 2 x 1.5cm balls and squash flat to create the eyes. Stick onto the cake using the glacé icing.

8 For the inner ears, use the remaining light-brown icing trimmings to mould 2 x 4cm oval shapes a little smaller than the ears. Place these on top of the darker ear shapes, then nip the 2 pieces of icing in at one end (picture E). Using glacé icing, stick the completed ears on the cake.

9 Roll the remaining chocolate icing into a large ball for the nose and separate smaller balls for the eyeballs. Attach with glacé icing. Using the fine paint brush, brush the chocolate buttons with glacé icing and attach around the base of the cake to create a collar.

10 To finish, roll the remaining white icing to 4mm thick and cut into a bow tie, using the template on p189; then use the back of a knife to add detail (picture F). Stick the bow tie to the cake with glacé icing.

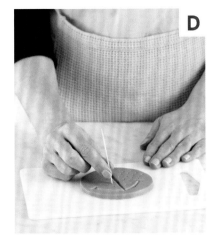

D

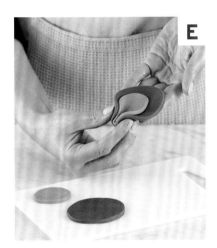

E

F

If you go down to the woods today...

The words to *Teddy Bears' Picnic* were written by Irish songwriter Jimmy Kennedy in 1932. He lived in Staplegrove, a parish of Taunton, Somerset. The magical bear-filled woods of the song are said to be located between Staplegrove Church, where Kennedy is buried, and the local Scout hut.

Special days

Valentine's Day cake

This romantic creation has a heart in every slice. What better way to seal your love?

RATING

SERVES 12

YOU WILL NEED
½ quantity Victoria sponge mixture, coloured with 1 tbsp cochineal red food colouring by Sainsbury's and baked in a 20cm square cake tin for 30 mins (see p14), cooled

Butter, for greasing

½ quantity Victoria sponge mixture, weighing exactly 500g (see p14)

¼ quantity biscuit dough (see p19)

½ quantity rich white chocolate buttercream (see p23)

1 quantity royal icing (see p24)

TO DECORATE
2 tbsp apricot glaze by Sainsbury's, warmed

2 tsp red food colouring

1 tsp pink food colouring

4 tsp icing sugar, plus extra if required

3 packs mini blossom cake decorations by Sainsbury's

80g bag princess milk chocolate hearts by Sainsbury's

YOU WILL ALSO NEED
5cm heart-shaped cutter by Sainsbury's

1 long rectangular cake plate

3 disposable piping bags

3 small round writing piping nozzles

1 fine paint brush

PER SERVING
808 cals, 33.8g fat, 19.3g sat fat, 97.5g total sugars, 0.29g salt

1 Place the pink square sponge cake on a surface and cut out 9 hearts with the cutter (picture A). Brush the hearts on one side with the apricot glaze and stick together to make a long heart-shaped cake (picture B). Transfer to the freezer and chill for 30 mins.

2 Preheat the oven to 180°C, fan 160°C, gas 4. Grease and line the base of a non-stick 2lb (900g) loaf tin with baking paper (see p20). Spoon 2-3 tbsp of the Victoria sponge mixture into the bottom of the loaf tin and spread it out in an even layer. Place the heart cake on top, pointed end facing upwards. Gently spoon the remaining sponge mixture around and over the heart cake, covering it fully (picture C). Don't worry if the heart looks as though it is sticking out slightly – the plain Victoria sponge mixture will rise during baking to cover it completely.

3 Bake for 45-50 mins until cooked through. Allow to cool with the loaf tin set upside down on a wire rack so the cake begins to come

TURN OVER FOR THE REMAINING RECIPE STEPS

Valentine's Day cake (continued)

away from the sides of the tin. You may need to run a knife around the edge of the cake to help it slide out.

4 Meanwhile, preheat the oven to 190°C, fan 170°C, gas 5. Roll out the biscuit dough to 4mm thick and cut out a heart shape, using the template on p191 (picture D). Place on a non-stick baking tray and bake in the preheated oven for 10 mins until beginning to turn golden around the edges. Set aside to cool on a wire rack. (You can use the dough trimmings to make extra biscuits.)

5 Cover the top and sides of the cooled upturned loaf cake with the white chocolate buttercream, then transfer to the fridge to chill for 15 mins.

6 Meanwhile, set aside 2 tbsp royal icing, then evenly divide the remainder between 3 bowls. Colour one bowl of icing with 1 tsp of the red colouring, another with the remaining 1 tsp red colouring and the third bowl with the pink colouring. Mix in 2 tsp icing sugar each to 1 bowl of red and the pink icing. This should thicken the icing and make it possible to pipe stripes onto the cake. If it isn't thick enough, continue to add teaspoons of icing sugar until you have the consistency you want. Spoon the thickened red and pink icings into separate disposable piping bags, each fitted with a small round writing piping nozzle.

7 Pipe a heart outline onto the cooled heart biscuit using the thickened red icing. Spoon the slightly looser red royal icing into the middle (picture E), then leave to set.

8 Meanwhile, pipe alternate red and pink coloured stripes onto the sides of the cake, starting from the top of the cake and finishing at the base. Finish with a little squeeze to create a small blob at the bottom of each stripe (picture F).

9 Brush the undersides of the mini blossom decorations with a little water and stick around the top edge of the cake, covering the start point of each of the piped stripes and overlapping slightly (picture G).

10 When the icing has set on the heart biscuit, put the 2 tbsp of set aside white royal icing into a disposable piping back fitted with a fine writing nozzle and pipe on a Valentine's message. Arrange the iced biscuit heart on the cake. Decorate the top of the cake with the princess chocolates and serve in slices so you can see the heart cake in the middle.

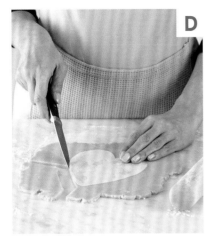

D

E

F

G

Easter chocolate cake

A rich chocolate cake topped with a decadent Easter egg sitting in its own chocolate nest

RATING

SERVES 20

YOU WILL NEED
1 quantity chocolate
sponge mixture baked
in 2 x 23cm round tins for
45 mins (see p16), cooled

1½ quantities rich white
chocolate buttercream
(see p23)

TO DECORATE
150g mini eggs

1½ x 125g packs chocolate
fingers, cut into rough
halves – they look better
if they're not exact

12 white wild rose cake
decorations by Sainsbury's

Fresh mint sprigs

3 Shredded Wheat
biscuits, crushed

200g dark chocolate,
melted (see p25)

25g milk chocolate,
peeled into shavings (with
a vegetable peeler)

1 medium chocolate Easter
egg (about 220g)

6 butterfly cake
decorations by Sainsbury's

YOU WILL ALSO NEED
1 large cake board
or plate

Beading or florist wire

PER SERVING
807 cals, 44.7g fat,
25.2g sat fat, 81.8g total
sugars, 0.41g salt

1 Trim the tops of the cakes with a serrated knife, if necessary, to make them even (see p21). Put one of the cakes upside down on a cake board and use a palette knife to spread the top with a thick layer of buttercream.

2 Reserve around 16 of the mini eggs, then put the remainder in a freezer bag and crush with a rolling pin (picture A). Put the crushed mini eggs on top of the first cake, then top with the other cake and spread half of the remaining buttercream over the top and sides of both cakes. Chill for 10-15 mins, then repeat with the remaining buttercream.

3 Press the halved chocolate fingers into the side of the cake to create a 'fence' (picture B). Press the white rose decorations into the buttercream above the 'fence' and insert a mint sprig beneath each flower.

4 Make the 'nest'. In a mixing bowl, stir the crushed Shredded Wheat (reserving a few strands) into the melted chocolate until coated (picture C), then spoon teaspoons of the mixture onto the centre of the cake in a ring shape. Scatter over the milk chocolate shavings and sprinkle over the reserved Shredded Wheat strands. Position the Easter egg in the centre of the 'nest'. Using a rolling pin, gently break 8 of the reserved mini eggs in half, then press them on the top of the cake and in the nest with the remaining whole eggs.

5 Cut 6 x 20cm lengths of beading or florist wire. Gently wind the top of each length around a butterfly and stick them into the top of the cake to finish (remove the wires when serving).

A

B

C

Mother's Day cake

A box of chocolates with a difference – this cake will show your mum just how special she is

RATING

SERVES 20

YOU WILL NEED
1 quantity chocolate sponge mixture baked in 2 x 20cm round cake tins for 40-45 mins (see p16), cooled

1 quantity rich chocolate buttercream (see p23)

TO DECORATE
60ml double cream

10g unsalted butter

75g dark chocolate

Icing sugar, for dusting

2 x 500g packs ready to roll chocolate flavour icing by Sainsbury's

250g pack ready to roll pink icing by Sainsbury's

25g chocolate coffee beans by Sainsbury's

25g red, pink and white 100s & 1000s, glimmer sugar and sugar hearts (from 90g pot princess sprinkles by Sainsbury's)

½ x 250g box Belgian chocolate seashells by Sainsbury's

YOU WILL ALSO NEED
2 gold cake ribbons by Sainsbury's

1 large round cake plate or board

1 fine paint brush

Melon baller or ½ tbsp metal measuring spoon

12 petits fours cases by Sainsbury's

Roll of double-sided sticky tape

PER SERVING
834 cals, 37.3g fat, 20g sat fat, 105.1g total sugars, 0.3g salt

1 To make the truffle mixture for the chocolates on top of the cake, gently warm the cream and butter together in a small pan over a low heat. Once the mixture is just steaming, remove from the heat. Break up the chocolate and stir into the hot cream mixture, until melted and smooth. Pour into a small freezer-proof glass bowl or container. Freeze for 1 hour, until solid.

2 Sandwich the risen sides of the cakes together with a quarter of the buttercream so you have a flat base and a flat top. Place on a chopping board and spread all but 2 tbsp of the remaining buttercream over the top and sides of the cake.

3 Dust a surface with icing sugar. Roll out 200g of the chocolate icing to a rough long, thin rectangle about 3mm thick (see tip, p97). Trim with a sharp knife to a 1.5cm x 62cm strip. Position around the top of the cake (picture A). Use the remaining buttercream to fill in any gaps between the cake and the icing strip.

TURN OVER FOR THE REMAINING RECIPE STEPS

94

Mother's Day cake (continued)

4 Re-roll the icing trimmings and the remaining 800g chocolate icing to a large 4mm-thick circle. It needs to be large enough to cover the cake and sides. Use a rolling pin to drape the icing over the cake. Smooth it down with the palms of your hands and run a finger around the inside of the raised lip to push the icing into place (picture B). Trim the excess icing from the base of the cake with a sharp knife (picture C).

5 Lay one of the cake ribbons across the middle of the cake plate. Carefully transfer the cake onto the cake plate and ribbon using two cake lifters or palette knives (picture D).

6 Roll out the pink icing to a rough rectangle about 3mm thick, then cut to a 12cm x 30cm rectangle. Use a ruler and a sharp knife to cut the rectangle into 12cm strips of varying widths: 5mm, 2cm and 2.5cm. Brush each strip with a little water and carefully stick onto the side of the cake (picture E), gently pressing over the raised icing lip. Trim with a sharp knife. Brush the chocolate coffee beans with a little water, then secure around the base of the cake to add a neat trim.

7 Take the frozen truffle mixture out of the freezer and let stand for 5-10 mins. Use the melon baller to scoop out little balls of the truffle mixture. If you're using a ½ tbsp metal measuring spoon, scoop out truffle halves, level with a knife and use a teaspoon to help release the halves, then press two together to make a ball.

8 Put the different sprinkles in separate shallow bowls, then toss the truffles in the different coloured sprinkles to coat (picture F). Put the truffles and chocolate seashells in petits fours cases and place on top of the cake. Carefully pull up the sides of the ribbon and secure with a small knot. Tie the second ribbon in a bow, trim and secure on top of the knot with double-sided sticky tape.

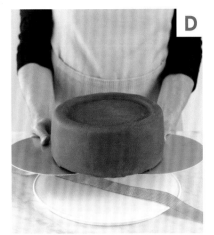

D

E

F

How do I roll out narrow strips of icing to an even thickness?

Roll the icing into a thick sausage shape and place between 2 x 3mm-thick chopping boards that have been dusted with icing sugar. Press down with a rolling pin over the top board until the desired thickness is achieved.

Father's Day shirt & tie cake

Give Dad a smart new shirt and tie on his special day - in the form of this tasty cake!

RATING

SERVES 24

YOU WILL NEED
1½ quantities Victoria sponge mixture baked in a 22cm x 32cm x 5cm deep rectangular baking tray for 1 hour 15 mins (see p14), cooled

½ quantity vanilla buttercream (see p22)

TO DECORATE
Icing sugar, for dusting

1.25kg ready to roll blue icing, kneaded together

250g ready to roll white icing

150g ready to roll red icing

25g ready to roll black icing

YOU WILL ALSO NEED
1 large rectangular cake board

1 fine paint brush

1 cocktail stick

Small alphabet cutters

PER SERVING
630 cals, 23.6g fat, 14.2g sat fat, 88.8g total sugars, 0.22g salt

1 Put the cake on the cake board and, if necessary, level the top with a serrated knife (see p21). Halve the cake horizontally and spread the bottom half with half of the buttercream. Sandwich the two halves together and spread the remaining buttercream in a thin layer over the top and sides of the cake.

2 Dust a surface with icing sugar and roll out the blue icing to a rectangle roughly 30cm x 42cm x 3mm thick. Use a rolling pin to drape the icing over the cake. Using your hands, smooth the icing around the sides and corners of the cake. If you have one, use a cake smoother, lightly dusted with icing sugar, to give the icing a very smooth finish, moving it in a circular motion all over the cake. Trim the excess icing from around the base of the cake and reserve the trimmings.

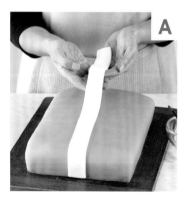

TURN OVER FOR THE REMAINING RECIPE STEPS

Father's Day shirt & tie cake (continued)

3 Roll out 75g of the white icing to 3mm thick and trim to a long, thin strip to run down the length of the cake. Roll out 25g of the white icing to 3mm thick and cut out a 6cm x 7cm rectangle for the breast pocket. Use a little of the red icing to shape a triangular handkerchief. Brush the icing strip, handkerchief and pocket with a little cooled boiled water and stick to the cake as shown (pictures A and B).

4 Shape 5 buttons from some of the reserved blue icing trimmings. Use a cocktail stick to make the holes, then attach 4 to the strip and 1 to the pocket with a dab of water. Dot the point of a cocktail stick around the edges of the strip and pocket to create 'stitching' (picture C).

5 Roll out the remaining white icing and trim to an 8cm x 28cm x 3mm-thick rectangle, then cut to an opened-out collar shape (see template on p191). Gently fold in half lengthways then curve into shape (picture D), brush the underside with a little water and attach to the cake to form a collar.

6 Dust a surface with icing sugar and roll out the black icing to 2mm thick. Cut out the word 'Dad' using small alphabet cutters (picture E) and attach to the inside of the collar with water.

7 Roll out the rest of the red icing to a long, thin rectangle approximately 10cm x 36cm x 3mm thick, then cut out a tie shape from the rectangle. Reserve the trimmings. Roll out the rest of the blue icing trimmings to 2mm thick and cut out 9 x 1cm x 12cm strips. Attach 8 of the strips to the tie with a little water to create a striped effect, then trim off the excess icing at the edges (picture F).

8 Drape the tie at an angle down the length and over one side of the cake, ruffling it a little in places (you may need to place some small rolls of kitchen paper under the ruffles until the icing is firm). Secure with a little water. Form a tie knot shape from the red icing trimmings and place at the top of the tie, securing with a dab of water. Secure the final blue strip across the knot, trimming to fit.

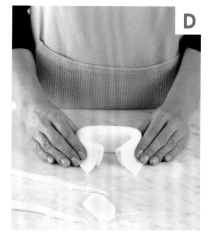

D

E

F

Knotty knowledge

The modern-day tie has its
origins in neckerchiefs worn
by Croatian soldiers in the
Thirty Years War of 1618-
1648. The trend caught on in
Paris, where the garment was
named the cravat, after Hrvati
(people from Croatia). During
the Industrial Revolution, ties
became thinner and more
like the ones we know today.

Halloween graveyard cake

Spooky gravestone biscuits, ghostly mice and creepy crawlies make this a brilliant fright night treat

RATING

SERVES 24

YOU WILL NEED
¹/₂ quantity biscuit dough
mixture (see p19), chilled

1¹/₂ quantities chocolate
sponge mixture baked in
a 22cm x 32cm x 5cm
deep rectangular baking
tray for 1 hour 15 mins
(see p16), cooled

1 quantity rich chocolate
buttercream (see p23)

TO DECORATE
75g pack strawberry laces
by Sainsbury's

Black writing icing
pen (from 76g pack
colour writing icing
by Sainsbury's)

2 bourbon cream
biscuits by Sainsbury's,
crushed

20g desiccated coconut

Few drops of green
food colouring

30g chocolate buttons
(use a mixture of milk and
white chocolate)

100g white chocolate

4 jelly sweets

2 white chocolate mice

YOU WILL ALSO NEED
1 large rectangular
cake board

1 cake pop stick
by Sainsbury's

PER SERVING
632 cals, 33.5g fat,
18.1g sat fat, 56.8g total
sugars, 0.39g salt

1 Preheat the oven to 190°C, fan 170°C, gas
5. Roll out the biscuit dough to 3mm thick,
then, using a sharp knife, cut out 3 gravestone
shapes and 1 cross (picture A). Put the shapes
on a non-stick baking sheet and bake for 10-12
mins, until golden. Allow to cool.

A

2 Cut the sponge in half horizontally. Put the
bottom half on the cake board and spread
with half the buttercream. Criss-cross most
of the laces on top, letting the ends hang
over the sides. Sandwich together with the
other half of cake (picture B). Spread the
remaining buttercream over the top.

B

3 Use the writing icing pen to write spooky
inscriptions on the biscuits and press into
the top of the cake. Scatter the crushed
bourbon biscuits around the 'gravestones'.

4 Mix the coconut and green food colouring
together in a bowl (picture C), then scatter
over the cake to look like grass.

C

5 Make a spooky worm by overlapping the
buttons in a line on top of the cake. Use the
writing icing pen to draw on eyes and a mouth.
Cut a piece of a remaining lace for a tongue.

6 To make the ghost, melt the white chocolate
(see p25). Cool slightly, then spoon over a cake
pop stick on a tray lined with baking paper.
Leave to harden, then use the writing icing pen
to make eyes and a mouth. Lift off the paper
and stick into the cake.

7 Make faces on the jelly sweets and eyes on the
white mice using the writing icing pen. Arrange
more strawberry laces over the gravestones.

Halloween pumpkin cake

Unlike the traditional carved pumpkin, this fabulous cake version will be eaten in its entirety!

RATING

SERVES 24

YOU WILL NEED
Sunflower oil, for greasing

1¹/₂ quantities chocolate sponge mixture (see p16)

1 quantity vanilla buttercream (see p22)

TO DECORATE
1 tbsp red food colouring

1 tbsp yellow food colouring

50g cocoa powder

1¹/₂ tbsp semi-skimmed milk

75g bourbon cream biscuits by Sainsbury's, whizzed to crumbs in a food processor

8 cola laces by Sainsbury's

Icing sugar, for dusting

25g ready to roll black icing

100g ready to roll green icing

YOU WILL ALSO NEED
1 large plate

1 large square cake board, platter or plate

1 wooden skewer, cut to 18cm long

PER SERVING
565 cals, 29g fat, 15.1g sat fat, 53.5g total sugars, 0.43g salt

1 Preheat the oven to 180ºC, fan 160ºC, gas 4. Grease and line an 18cm loose-bottomed round deep cake tin with baking paper (see p20).

2 Grease a 750ml round Pyrex bowl with a little sunflower oil, and place a 3cm disc of baking paper in the bottom. Pour in 275g of the cake mixture and cook in the microwave at 360W for 6 mins. Remove from the microwave and immediately turn out onto a wire rack, taking care as the cake will be very hot. Repeat using another 275g of the mixture, and set both cakes aside to cool completely.

3 Meanwhile, pour the remaining cake mix into the prepared 18cm tin and bake in the oven for 1 hour 20 mins or until a skewer comes out clean. Leave to cool in the tin for 10 mins, then turn out onto a wire rack to cool completely.

4 Take a third of the buttercream and transfer to another bowl. Beat the red and yellow food

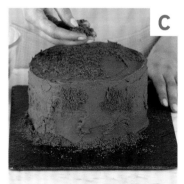

TURN OVER FOR THE REMAINING RECIPE STEPS

Halloween pumpkin cake (continued)

colouring into this smaller portion to get a vibrant orange colour, then beat the cocoa powder and milk into the remaining two-thirds of the buttercream.

5 Once they are cool, set one of the 2 microwave cake halves, rounded side down, onto the large upturned plate. Spread a little of the orange buttercream on top (picture A) and put the other half of the cake on top to form a ball. Using a palette knife, cover the ball with orange icing (picture B), chill in the fridge for 10-15 mins, then coat again to hide any cake crumbs. Finish with vertical sweeping motions to give the look of pumpkin skin.

6 Using a long serrated knife, level the top of the large round cake (see p21) and place on the cake board, platter or flat cake plate. Cover the cake with a layer of chocolate buttercream, then sparingly sprinkle and pat the crushed bourbon biscuits over the top and sides (picture C), leaving enough exposed buttercream to stick on the leaves and vines.

7 Push the wooden skewer vertically into the centre of the cake. Push two forks into the bottom third of the pumpkin cake and carefully lift and lower it onto the skewer (picture D) to secure in place. Smooth over any smudged icing with a palette knife once the pumpkin is in place. Decorate with the cola laces (picture E), snipping off the excess with scissors.

8 Dust a surface with icing sugar and roll out the black icing to 3mm thick. Using the template on p190, cut out the eyes, nose and mouth of the pumpkin and stick them in place on the buttercream. Roll out the green icing to 3mm thick and use a sharp knife to cut out leaves. Score on veins with a knife (picture F). Use the green icing trimmings to make the pumpkin stalk. Roll 30g of the icing into a ball, then flatten it slightly and make a dent in it with your thumb. Roll another 10g into a stalk shape, then stick it to the flattened ball with a little water. Place on the top of the pumpkin. Roll the rest of the green icing into thin sausage shapes for the vines, then arrange the leaves and vines around the base of the pumpkin.

Veggie vigilante

Although the origins of carving gourds and squashes into jack-o'-lanterns at Halloween are shrouded in mystery, it's thought the practice may have started in Ireland, where lanterns were often made from turnips. The smiling, slightly sinister lanterns are supposed to protect homes from vampires and the 'undead'.

Bonfire cake

This sizzling creation will add plenty of sparkle to your 5th November celebrations

RATING

SERVES 15

YOU WILL NEED
1/2 quantity chocolate sponge mixture baked in a 20cm round cake tin for 40-45 mins (see p16), cooled

1 quantity chocolate ganache (see p22)

TO DECORATE
1 orange, peel only

450g caster sugar

50g dark chocolate

95g basics chocolate Swiss roll, 1.5cm removed from one end (cook's treat)

167g box chocolate crunchy orange sticks by Sainsbury's

25g white chocolate, grated

125g ready to roll red icing

125g ready to roll yellow icing

125g ready to roll chocolate flavour icing

1 tsp apricot glaze by Sainsbury's, warmed

YOU WILL ALSO NEED
25cm round gold cake board by Sainsbury's

Cocktail sticks

Selection of leaf-shaped cutters (optional)

PER SERVING
610 cals, 25.1g fat, 13.9g sat fat, 81g total sugars, 0.27g salt

1 Slice the orange peel into 5mm strips, leaving the pith on. Place in a small saucepan of water and bring to the boil, then drain and repeat. Return the peel to the pan with 150ml fresh water and 300g of the caster sugar. Simmer for 40 mins, then remove from the syrup and leave to dry overnight on a wire rack.

2 Make the caramel shards. Line a baking tray with baking paper. Pour the remaining 150g caster sugar into a saucepan and place over a low heat. Shake the pan a little until the sugar starts to clump together – it will slowly turn a caramel colour. Keep it on the heat until fully melted, then pour onto the baking paper. Set aside to cool. Once cold and completely hard, break the caramel into shards to create bonfire 'flames'. Set aside.

3 Peel off 30g dark chocolate shavings using a vegetable peeler (picture A). Set the remaining chocolate aside in the fridge.

4 Put the cooled round sponge on the cake board. Insert 3 cocktail sticks vertically into the

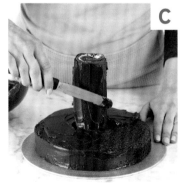

TURN OVER FOR THE REMAINING RECIPE STEPS

Bonfire cake (continued)

middle of the cake and secure the Swiss roll on top, standing it vertically (picture B). Spread the ganache over the cake and chocolate Swiss roll (picture C).

5 Heat the remaining 20g dark chocolate in the microwave on a low heat for 2 mins until melted, stirring halfway through. Dip the flat side of a crunchy orange stick into the chocolate and place it onto another stick at a slight angle, using the chocolate as glue. Repeat with three-quarters of the orange sticks, making pairs of 'bundled twigs'. Reserve the remaining whole sticks. Lay the joined twig bundles on a plate, then put them in the fridge for 20 mins to set.

6 Scatter the grated white chocolate and dark chocolate shavings on the base cake around the Swiss roll. Take the joined twig bundles out of the fridge and arrange them around the

Swiss roll to form a 'bonfire' (picture D). Break some of the remaining crunchy sticks in half and poke these out of the top of the Swiss roll. Arrange the remaining whole sticks around the cake. Poke in the orange peel and caramel shards to create 'flames' between the sticks.

7 Marble together a little of the red and yellow icings and shape into more flames (picture E). Add these to the bonfire - you can also wrap them around any remaining crunchy sticks for a good flame effect.

8 To decorate the side of the cake and the board, roll out the remaining red and yellow icing and the chocolate flavour icing as thinly as you can to make leaves and flowers. Use a sharp knife or cookie cutters to form the shapes. Brush apricot glaze onto the back of the shapes and stick them around the cake and onto the board to finish (picture F).

Remember, remember...
Bonfire Night commemorates
the plot, culminating on 5
November 1605, to blow up the
House of Lords and kill King
James I. One of the plotters,
Guy Fawkes, was caught and
the plot was foiled, sparking
bonfire celebrations. Until
1859, the date was an official
day of remembrance, known
as Gunpowder Treason Day.

Simple Christmas cake

Celebrate the festive season with this traditional fruit cake decorated with stars, holly and ivy and finished with pretty red ribbon

RATING 🧁

SERVES 16

YOU WILL NEED
1 quantity fruit cake mixture baked in a 20cm round deep tin for 4 hours (see p18), cooled

TO DECORATE
2 tbsp apricot glaze by Sainsbury's, warmed

Icing sugar, for dusting

454g pack golden marzipan by Sainsbury's

1kg pack ready to roll white icing by Sainsbury's

1 tsp brandy

Glacé icing, for sticking (see p22)

2 tsp red sprinkles by Sainsbury's

50g ready to roll green icing (for the decorations, see p32)

1 tsp red pearls (from 69g pack red, blue & white pearls by Sainsbury's)

3 tbsp white shimmer pearls by Sainsbury's

YOU WILL ALSO NEED
1 large round cake plate

1 medium and 1 small star-shaped cutter

Leaf, ivy and flower cutters (to make the decorations, see p32 for more details)

1 fine paint brush

3 or 4 lengths of thin red ribbon

PER SERVING
817 cals, 22.9g fat, 9.8g sat fat, 130.9g total sugars, 0.09g salt

1 Brush the top and side of the cake with the apricot glaze.

2 Dust a surface with icing sugar and roll out the marzipan to 3mm thick, so you have roughly a 36cm circle. Use a rolling pin to drape the marzipan over the cake (picture A), smooth down all over to make an even surface, then trim the excess marzipan from the base.

3 Repeat step 2 with the white icing, rolling to 4mm thick and brushing the marzipan with brandy just before applying the icing to help it stick to the cake. Reserve the icing trimmings.

4 Put the cake on a large round cake board or plate. Roll out the white icing trimmings to 3mm thick. Using the star cutters, cut 3 outlines of stars (picture B) and 3 whole stars. Stick them onto the cake using a little glacé icing to secure. Fill the star outlines with the red sprinkles (picture C).

5 Make the holly, flowers and leaves from the remaining white icing, the green icing and some of the white pearls (see p32 for instructions) and stick on the cake by brushing with a little glacé icing. Gently press the red pearls into the base of the holly leaves to make berries.

6 Gently press the remaining white pearls into the white icing, around the stars, flowers and leaves. Position the ribbons around the side of the cake, criss-crossing over, and secure with a little glacé icing.

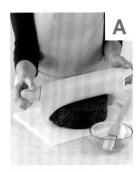

A

B

C

Christmas house cake

Celebrate the festive season with a magical wintry cottage that tastes as good as it looks

RATING

SERVES 34

YOU WILL NEED
2 quantities chocolate sponge mixture: ³/4 of the mixture baked in a 22cm x 32cm x 5cm deep rectangular baking tray for 1 hour 15 mins; the rest baked in a 2lb (900g) loaf tin for 45 mins (see p16), cooled

1 quantity vanilla buttercream (see p22)

200g chocolate ganache (see p22)

1 quantity royal icing (see p24)

TO DECORATE
150g ready to roll yellow icing

600g ready to roll white icing

Icing sugar, for dusting

167g pack chocolate crunchy mint sticks by Sainsbury's

2 x 200g packs dark chocolate mint thins by Sainsbury's

75g ready to roll black icing

100g ready to roll red icing

250g pack ready to roll green icing by Sainsbury's

¹/4 x 45g pot sparkle snowflakes by Sainsbury's

12 holly Christmas cake decorations by Sainsbury's

1 snowman icing figure by Sainsbury's (or make our alternative on p34)

¹/2 x 79g pot chocolate beans by Sainsbury's

YOU WILL ALSO NEED
1 large rectangular cake board

1 disposable piping bag

1 fine writing piping nozzle

PER SERVING
733 cals, 34.4g fat, 19.5g sat fat, 84.7g total sugars, 0.61g salt

1 Trim the rectangular cake so the sides are straight. Place on a chopping board and cut 2 x 11cm-wide pieces of cake from one end. Cut the remaining piece into 3 even-size pieces – one for the chimney, one for the porch and the other is a cook's treat! Cut a triangular wedge from the bottom of the chimney piece (picture A). This will form the roof of the porch. Sandwich the 2 x 11cm pieces together with some of the buttercream, one on top of the other, to form the main 'body' of the house.

2 Using a serrated knife, level the surface of the loaf cake if necessary (see p21), then cut it diagonally across lengthways (picture B). Flip the pieces over to make a triangle (picture C), then sandwich together with some buttercream to make the roof.

3 Put the house part of the cake on a large cake board and coat the top and sides with most of the remaining buttercream. Coat the porch piece with the rest of the buttercream and set aside.

TURN OVER FOR THE REMAINING RECIPE STEPS ▶

Christmas house cake (continued)

4 Knead the yellow and white icings together well to make a pale yellow. Dust a surface with icing sugar and roll the icing out to 4mm thick to give a rectangular shape big enough to cover the house cake. Use a rolling pin to drape the icing over the cake, then smooth down all over to create an even surface. Trim any excess icing from the base. Re-roll the trimmings to 3mm thick and use to cover the porch. Brush one side of the porch with a little water and press against the front of the house to attach.

5 Spread most of the chocolate ganache over the roof and dot some on top of the main part of the house. You will need to set some aside for the chimney and the porch roof. Carefully lift the roof using 2 large palette knives and position it on the house.

6 Put the chimney in place (fitting the triangular side into the roof) and coat with some of the remaining ganache. Gently press the crunchy mint sticks into the roof sides, cutting them to size as you go. (Use the offcuts for the corners.)

7 Press a row of chocolate mint thins along the bottom of one side of the roof, then continue to the top overlapping the rows as you go. Repeat on the other side (picture D). Use a small palette knife to smooth the ganache on the chimney and add some detail.

8 To make the porch roof, spread the remaining ganache over the triangular piece of cake, then decorate with small pieces of crunchy mint sticks at the front and two chocolate mint thins for the sides, then position carefully on the porch, sealing with a little ganache.

9 Gently knead together 25g of each of the black, red and green icings until the colours are marbled. Dust a surface with icing sugar and roll out to 2mm thick, then cut out 4 window shapes, each about 4cm x 5cm. Roll out 25g red icing to 2mm thick and cut out a 4cm x 5cm door. Using the back of a knife, lightly score on some lines to make the door panels, then roll a small piece of black icing into a ball and press onto the door for the doorknob. Attach the door and windows to the cake using a little water (picture E), then add a piece of mint stick for the doorstep.

10 Spoon a quarter of the royal icing into a piping bag fitted with a fine writing nozzle. Pipe on window frame details and icicles around the top of the chimney, the edge of the roof and the porch. Use small dots of royal icing to attach some of the snowflake sparkles around the edge of the roof and the chimney, the holly decorations above the porch and on the corners of the house.

11 Use the remaining red and black icings to roll and mould Santa's legs and boots, joining them together with a little of the royal icing (picture F). Put the legs in place on top of the chimney. Use the remaining green icing, the silver lustre and some of the chocolate beans and snowflake sparkles to make the Christmas trees (see p35 for details).

12 Use the remaining royal icing to coat the cake board (picture G), making 'peaks' with the back of a spoon. Push chocolate beans into the icing around the door to create Christmas lights. Add the snowman and Christmas trees, and finish with a dusting of icing sugar 'snow'.

D

E

F

G

Cakes with love

Daisy wedding cake

A stunningly romantic traditional three-tier wedding cake with a cascade of pretty daises

RATING 🧁🧁🧁

SERVES 90

YOU WILL NEED
¹/₂ quantity fruit cake mixture baked in a 12cm deep square tin for 2 hours (see p18), cooled

1 quantity fruit cake mixture baked in an 18cm deep square tin for 3 hours (see p18), cooled

1 ¹/₂ quantities fruit cake mixture baked in a 23cm deep square tin for 3¹/₂ hours (see p18), cooled

¹/₂ quantity royal icing (see p24)

TO DECORATE
250g pack white flower & modelling paste by Sainsbury's

Icing sugar, for dusting

6 x 454g packs golden marzipan by Sainsbury's

4 tbsp apricot glaze by Sainsbury's, warmed

6 x 500g packs ready to roll ivory icing by Sainsbury's

A few drops of yellow food colouring

YOU WILL ALSO NEED
1 set of 4 flower plunger cutters

Small piece of foam (a new foam scouring pad is ideal)

Small ball cake modelling tool (see p11)

1 x 12cm, 1 x 18cm and 1 x 23cm thin square cake boards

1 x 25cm x 12mm thick square cake board

2 x 30cm plastic cake dowels

3.5m x 13mm ivory satin ribbon

2 disposable piping bags

2 small round writing nozzles

PER SERVING
536 cals, 14.8g fat, 5.3g sat fat, 86.5g total sugars, 0.04g salt

1 Make the daises. Working with 50g white flower & modelling paste at a time, knead the paste until smooth. Roll out on a surface dusted with icing sugar to about 1mm thick. Using the flower plunger cutters, stamp out a few different-sized daisies. Place one daisy on a small piece of foam and, using the small ball cake modelling tool, curl each petal by smoothing the icing from the outside to the centre. Put the flower on a baking tray lined with baking paper and repeat with the rest of the daisies (picture A). Continue making daisies until you have about 325 in total – about 13 large, 55 medium, 130 small and 127 very small. Leave to dry overnight. Store in airtight boxes and handle gently.

2 To cover the cakes with marzipan you will need 450g for the 12cm cake, 850g for the 18cm cake and 1.3 kg for the 23cm cake. First, cover the 12cm cake. Spread a little royal icing over the 12cm thin square board and invert the 12cm cake onto it. Roll a little marzipan into thin sausage shapes and use to fill any gaps between the base

A

B

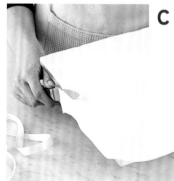

C

TURN OVER FOR THE REMAINING RECIPE STEPS ▶

Daisy wedding cake (continued)

of the cake and the board (picture B). Brush the cake all over with apricot glaze.

3 Dust a surface with icing sugar and roll out the rest of the first 454g pack of marzipan to a 28cm x 3mm thick square. Using a rolling pin, lift and drape it over the 12cm cake. Gently smooth down the marzipan around the sides of the cake. Trim away the excess with a knife.

4 Repeat with the other two cakes (placing them on the 18cm and 23cm square thin boards). Roll the marzipan to a 30cm square for the 18cm cake and a 35cm square for the 23cm cake. Leave in a cool place to dry for 1-2 days.

5 Roll out 400g ivory icing to a 30cm x 3mm thick square. Brush the 25cm cake board with cooled boiled water, then lift and lay the icing on the board. Smooth with a cake smoother and trim the excess icing around the board (picture C). Leave to dry overnight.

6 To ice the cakes with the ivory icing, you will need 500g for the 12cm cake, 750g for the 18cm cake and 1.25kg for the 23cm cake. First, cover the 12cm cake. Dust a surface with icing sugar and roll out the icing to a 30cm x 5mm thick square. Brush the marzipan-covered cake with cooled boiled water. Using a rolling pin, carefully lift the ivory icing and drape it over the cake, smoothing it down around the sides of the cake. Trim the excess icing with a knife. Repeat with the other two cakes. Roll the icing to a 32cm square for the 18cm cake and a 40cm square for the 23cm cake. Leave in a cool place to dry overnight.

7 To assemble, spread a little royal icing over the iced 25cm board and position the large square

cake in the centre. Mark a 17cm square on top of the cake with the tip of a knife. Insert a dowel into one corner, just inside the square, and mark it with a serrated knife to show the height of the cake (picture D). Remove the dowel and use the knife to cut through it on the mark. Push it back into the cake – it should be level with the top of the cake. Cut three further dowels to the length of the first one and push back into the three remaining corners of the square (this will stop the tiers sinking). Repeat for the second tier of the cake, marking an 11cm square.

8 Spread a little royal icing over the centre of the large cake and position the second cake on top. Attach ivory ribbon around the base of each cake, securing with a dab of the royal icing.

9 Halve the remaining royal icing. Take half and add yellow food colouring a drop at a time to make a pale yellow colour. Spoon into a piping bag fitted with a small round writing nozzle. Spoon the remaining white icing into a second piping bag fitted with a small round nozzle.

10 Decorate the four corners of the bottom and middle tiers with daisies. Use a dot of white icing to attach each daisy to the cake, pressing gently in the centre with your fingertip (picture E). Attach daisies all over the top of the 12cm cake and down each corner in the same way (picture F). Using the yellow icing, pipe a small dot into the centre of each daisy (picture G).

11 Spread a little white royal icing over the centre of the marked square on the middle tier and gently position the top tier in place. Attach a few small daisies to the board around the base of the cake to finish.

Ruffle wedding cake

Wow reception guests with this stunning wedding cake decorated with icing ruffles and roses

RATING 🧁 🧁 🧁

SERVES 70

YOU WILL NEED
2 quantities chocolate sponge mixture baked in 2 x 23cm deep round cake tins for 1 hour 15 mins (see p16), cooled

1 quantity chocolate sponge mixture baked in 2 x 18cm deep round cake tins for 45 mins (see p16), cooled

1/2 quantity chocolate sponge mixture baked in 2 x 15cm deep round cake tins for 30-35 mins (see p16), cooled

2 quantities vanilla buttercream (see p22)

TO DECORATE
Icing sugar, for dusting

1kg pack ready to roll white icing by Sainsbury's

4 x 250g packs modelling paste by Sainsbury's

1 1/4 tsp pink food colouring

2 tsp silver lustre

YOU WILL ALSO NEED
1 x 15cm thin round cake board

1 x 18cm thin round cake board

1 x 23cm thin round cake board

1 fine paint brush

8 cake pop sticks by Sainsbury's

1 large round cake plate or board

Plastic mini fondant rolling pin

Clear plastic A4 pocket (from stationery suppliers)

Cocktail sticks (optional)

PER SERVING
502 cals, 21.8g fat, 11.3g sat fat, 60.1g total sugars, 0.3g salt

1 Trim the cakes to get a flat surface, if necessary (see p21). You will be tiering the cake as seen in picture A. Sandwich 2 x 15cm cakes together with an even layer of the buttercream, then place on the 15cm cake board and spread an even layer of the buttercream over the top and sides of the cakes. Repeat with the 18cm cakes and board and the 23cm cakes and board.

2 Dust a surface with icing sugar. Roll out 150g white icing to about 15cm x 3mm thick circle. Use a rolling pin to drape the icing over the top of the cake, then smooth down to make an even surface. Trim the edges. Repeat with 200g icing for the 18cm cake and 300g for the 23cm cake. Wrap the sides of each cake in cling film to prevent drying out while you roll out the ruffled icing strips.

3 Mix 1 pack of the modelling paste with 70g white icing, kneading well, then wrap in cling film. Repeat with 2 more packs of modelling paste and 2 x 70g icing. This helps to keep the icing for the ruffles from drying out too quickly.

A

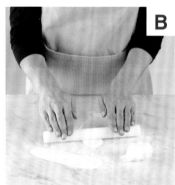

B

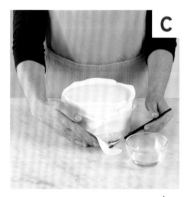

C

TURN OVER FOR THE REMAINING RECIPE STEPS ▶

Ruffle wedding cake (continued)

4 To make the ruffles, take a small ball of about 20g-30g from the modelling paste and icing mixture. Shape into a thin log, then roll out to a very thin strip, about 1-2mm thick using the mini rolling pin (picture B). It should measure about 18cm-24cm long and 5cm-6cm wide. The wavier the edges, the better!

5 Remove the cling film from the sides of the 15cm cake. Brush along the bottom half of the icing strip with a little cooled boiled water, and wrap the ruffle around the top edge of the cake. Position it so about a quarter of the ruffle comes over the top of the cake. Press with the palm of your hand to attach the ruffle to the cake, smoothing it down gently. Use a soft dry paint brush to gently curl out the top and edges of the ruffle. Repeat with more balls of modelling/icing paste until the cake is covered with ruffles, overlapping each one slightly (picture C). Trim the ends of some of the ruffles before attaching to the cake, then curl the corners slightly. When you reach the bottom of the cake, trim one side of the ruffles to give you a straight edge to line up with the bottom of the cake. If the ruffles don't stick on well, dab with a little more water using a fine paint brush.

6 For the middle and bottom tiers you will need to insert the cake pop sticks into the centre of each cake, cut to size, to support the layer above it. Starting with the middle cake, cut 4 cake pop sticks to the same lengths (to the height of the cake), then push them into the cake to form the corners of a square in the centre of the cake, where the layer above will sit. Make sure they are not too close together. Repeat with the bottom tier.

7 Place the top tier of the cake onto the middle tier (picture D) and repeat the process of making the ruffles and sticking them on. Then place the middle and top tiers onto the bottom tier and repeat the ruffle process again.

8 Mix together 1 tsp pink food colouring with the silver lustre. With the fine paint brush, carefully brush along the top edge of each ruffle, colouring the edges. Leave overnight to dry.

9 For the roses, mix the last pack of modelling paste with the remaining ¼ tsp pink food colouring, adding a small drop at a time and kneading in fully before adding the next drop.

10 To make the large roses, take 40g of the coloured sugar paste and roll out into a short log. Trim the ends and discard, then cut into 7 discs, about 3mm thick. Roll each disc out to about a 4cm diameter circle with the mini rolling pin (picture E). To get a really smooth shiny surface on the petals, roll them out in between an A4 clear plastic pocket.

11 Roll one of the discs up tightly to create the centre of your rose. Wrap the second petal over the seam of the first disc. Gently curl the top edge of the petal down. Continue to layer up the discs, creating the rose. Put each new petal over the seam of the one before. Once all petals are added, pinch the bottom of the rose together firmly and neaten the base with a knife to get a flat area. Repeat with the modelling paste to make 4 large roses. Set aside for 3-4 hours to dry.

12 For the small roses, repeat the above process using only 5 petals (picture F). Put the large and small roses around the cake, securing, if necessary, with cocktail sticks.

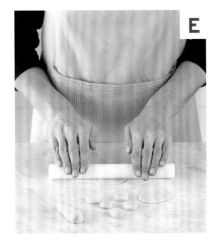

Colour me happy

It's simple to change the colours on this cake. Simply choose one of the many other food colourings Sainsbury's sells instore and online and match the quantities we have used in this recipe.

Happy anniversary cake

Celebrate a special date with this elegant anniversary cake

RATING 🧁 🧁

SERVES 16

YOU WILL NEED
1 quantity chocolate sponge mixture baked in a 20cm square cake tin for 1 hour-1 hour 15 mins (see p16), cooled

1 quantity vanilla buttercream (see p22)

1 quantity royal icing (see p24)

TO DECORATE
1-2 tsp icing sugar, plus extra to dust

1kg pack ready to roll white icing by Sainsbury's

2 tsp white shimmer pearls by Sainsbury's

2 tbsp silver balls

1 pack silver edible lustre by Sainsbury's

YOU WILL ALSO NEED
1 large, thick square silver cake board

6cm round cutter

2 disposable piping bags

1 writing piping nozzle

1 large round piping nozzle

PER SERVING
912 cals, 34.6g fat, 18.5g sat fat, 127.3g total sugars, 0.4g salt

1 Put the cake on the cake board and level the top if necessary (see p21). Turn upside down so the flat bottom of the cake is uppermost. Halve horizontally, then sandwich the 2 halves together with half the buttercream. Spread the rest of the buttercream in an even layer over the top and sides of the cake.

2 Dust a surface with icing sugar and roll out the white icing to about 36cm square x 4mm thick. Use a rolling pin to drape the icing over the cake, then smooth down to make an even surface. Trim the edges, reserving the trimmings.

3 Roll the trimmings out to 5mm thick. Using the 6cm round cutter, stamp out 2 circles and cut 2 thin 4.5cm x 5mm long strips for the stems of the glasses. Cut a semi-circle off the top of each circle (about 2cm in depth) and trim to a triangle for the base of the glasses (picture A).

4 Score a curved line in each 'glass' with the tip of a knife and press a few of the pearls and silver balls into the icing just above the line. Paint the glass, stems and bases with lustre.

5 Spoon a quarter of the royal icing into a piping bag fitted with the thin writing nozzle. Attach the glasses to the cake with a little of the icing. Press the rest of the pearls and half the remaining silver balls into icing around the glasses to resemble overflowing bubbles.

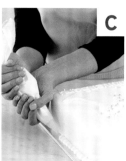

6 Pipe the words onto the cake (picture B). Add 1-2 tsp icing sugar to the remaining royal icing to thicken, then spoon the icing into a piping bag fitted with the large round nozzle. Pipe a shell border around the cake base (picture C) and dot with the rest of the silver balls.

Gift box cake

A stack of pretty gift boxes makes a stunning cake for a special birthday

RATING

SERVES 40

YOU WILL NEED
1¹/₂ quantities chocolate sponge mixture baked in 1 x 23cm square deep cake tin for 1¹/₂ hours (see p16), cooled

1 quantity rich white chocolate buttercream (see p23)

1 quantity chocolate sponge mixture baked in 2 x 15cm square cake tins for 1 hour (see p16), cooled

TO DECORATE
Icing sugar, for dusting

4 x 250g packs ready to roll blue icing by Sainsbury's, kneaded together

1kg pack ready to roll white icing by Sainsbury's

3 x 250g packs ready to roll pink icing by Sainsbury's, kneaded together

YOU WILL ALSO NEED
1 large square cake board

1 fine paint brush

3cm round cutter

1 large round piping nozzle

1 x 15cm square thin cake board

PER SERVING
743 cals, 29.2g fat, 15.2g sat fat, 98.9g total sugars, 0.38g salt

1 For this cake, the large sponge forms the bottom box, while the two smaller sponges form the top box and its lid (picture A). Place the 23cm cake on the large square cake board and, if necessary, level the top with a serrated knife (see p21). Halve horizontally and spread with a quarter of the buttercream and sandwich back together. Spread a third of the remaining buttercream in a thin, even layer over the top and sides of the large cake.

2 Dust a surface with icing sugar and roll out the blue icing to about 40cm square x 3mm thick. Use a rolling pin to drape the icing over the cake, then smooth down to make an even surface. Use a cake smoother, lightly dusted with icing sugar, to give the icing a very smooth finish, moving it in a circular motion all over the cake. Trim the excess icing from around the base of the cake with a sharp knife.

3 To make the bow, roll out 50g of the white icing to 3mm thick, and cut it to a 5cm x 15cm strip. Brush along the centre and 2 ends of the

A

B

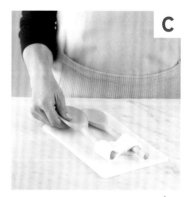

C

TURN OVER FOR THE REMAINING RECIPE STEPS

Gift box cake (continued)

strip with a little cooled boiled water, then fold the edges to meet in the centre (picture B). Pinch the icing together in the centre to create a bow shape. Roll a thin strip of icing from the trimmings and wrap it around the pinched section, using a little water to help it stick. Put the bow on a board and slide the handles of 2 wooden spoons between the loops to help separate them (picture C).

4 To make the ribbon, roll out another 50g of the white icing to 3mm thick. Cut 3 strips measuring 13cm x 2.5cm. Arrange them on the corner of the large cake (as shown in the main picture on the previous page) and attach to the large cake with a dab of cooled, boiled water.

5 Roll out 75g of white icing to 1mm-2mm thick and stamp out about 25 small dots with a 3cm cutter (or use the widest end of the large piping nozzle). Attach to the cake with a dab of water (picture D) - you won't need to put any of the polka dots on the part of the cake where the second cake will be positioned.

6 Trim the 15cm cakes, if necessary (see p21), then sandwich them together with half of the remaining buttercream. Put onto the thin cake board and cover with the remaining buttercream. Roll out the remaining white icing to 3mm thick and use a rolling pin to drape the icing over the cake (making sure you cover the edge of the cake board) and smooth it down with the palms of your hands. Trim the excess icing with a sharp knife. Reserve the trimmings to make the loops for the top of the cake.

7 Line a shallow tray with baking paper. Roll out 50g of the pink icing to 1-2mm thick. Using the narrow end of the large round nozzle, cut out 88 x 1cm wide circles. The best way to get them out is to turn the nozzle upside down and tap on the opposite end so the icing circle falls out. Put the circles onto the lined tray to dry.

8 For the lid of the box, roll out 500g pink icing to 3mm thick. Cut to 23cm square (reserving the trimmings) and gently lift onto the top of your box, making sure the sides are all even. Trim the pink icing with a knife so that it comes about 3-4cm down the sides of the cake from the top, reserving the trimmings (picture E). Be careful not to cut into the white icing underneath. Using a little water, stick the pink dots onto the rest of the white box.

9 Roll out the remaining pink icing to 3mm thick and cut into 15 x 2cm wide x 12cm long strips. Fold each strip in half and stick together at the ends with a little water. Cut the stuck-together ends into points to make it easier to fit them onto the top of the cake. Thread the loops onto the handles of 2 dry wooden spoons to keep their shape. Repeat with the same quantity of white icing to make another 15 loops.

10 Leave all the iced cakes, bow, loops and ribbons in a cool dry place overnight to allow the icing to dry.

11 To assemble, place the small cake on top of the large cake at an angle. Remove the wooden spoons from the bow and attach it next to the ribbons with a little cooled, boiled water. For the gift bow, layer the icing loops on top of the small cake, starting with 8 loops on the bottom layer, then continuing with layers of 7 and 6 and 2 loops. Use a little water to secure them as you go. You can practise on a work surface first to get the shape right (picture F).

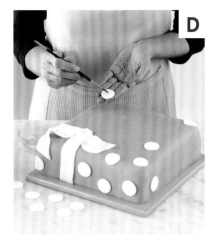

D

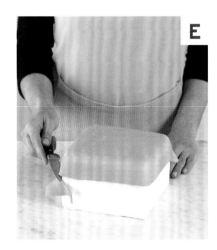

E

F

Going dotty

Polka dots first came into vogue in the 19th century, when the dance that shares the same name became popular. Beloved of Flamenco dancers and itsy-bitsy teeny-weeny yellow bikini wearers alike, they've never gone out of style. In the 1960s there was even a comic-book villain called Polka-Dot Man!

New baby cake

Celebrate a new baby or christening with this impressive cake topped with Battenberg blocks

RATING 🧁

SERVES 24

YOU WILL NEED
1 quantity Victoria sponge mixture baked in 2 x 23cm round cake tins for 30 mins (see p14), cooled

1 quantity vanilla buttercream (see p22)

TO DECORATE
A few drops of yellow food colouring

500g pack ready to roll white icing by Sainsbury's

Icing sugar, for dusting

250g packs each blue, green, yellow and red ready to roll icings by Sainsbury's (for the additional decorations, see p33-34 for details)

White writing icing pen (from 76g pack chocolate & caramel flavoured writing icing by Sainsbury's)

4 x 220g Battenberg cakes, halved to make 8 square blocks in total

YOU WILL ALSO NEED
1 large cake plate

Medium-size alphabet shape cutters

Various shapes from the mini cookie cutter set by Sainsbury's

2 long wooden skewers, trimmed to between 20-25cm

PER SERVING
671 cals, 26g fat, 13.3g sat fat, 90g total sugars, 0.32g salt

1 If necessary, trim the tops of the cakes (see p21), then sandwich together using about a third of the buttercream. Spread the rest over the top and sides of the cake. Transfer to a plate.

2 Make the yellow blanket. Knead the yellow food colouring into the white icing, one drop at a time, until the icing turns an even, pale yellow (picture A). Dust a surface with icing sugar and roll out the icing to a large circle, 38cm x 4mm thick. Use a rolling pin to drape the icing over the cake. Smooth out the icing on the top of the cake, then shape a 'skirt' around the sides (picture B).

3 Make the baby blocks. Dust a surface with icing sugar. Roll out half of each of the coloured icings to 2mm thick. With a knife, cut 5 x 5mm wide strips from each. Cut to size to make the borders of your blocks. Use alphabet cutters to stamp out letters to spell 'It's a boy', or 'It's a girl', and the mini cookie cutters for other shapes. Use the white chocolate writing icing (from the writing icing pack) to fix the borders, shapes and letters to the Battenberg halves.

4 Push the skewers down into the cake on opposite sides, then push the blocks onto the skewers to secure into place and spell out your message. If your cake is for a boy, put only stars on the extra block and place it on the other side of the cake. Place the 'A' block between the two towers, securing it with a little writing icing.

5 Shape little bears, ducklings (see p32-33 for details) and additional icing blocks from the remaining icing and use as extra decorations.

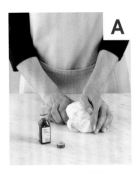

A

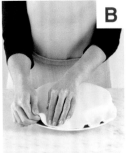

B

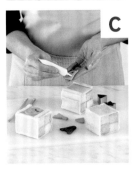

C

Congratulations cake

You'll be as happy as can be with this celebratory masterpiece

RATING

SERVES 24

YOU WILL NEED

1½ quantities Victoria sponge mixture (see p14)

½ quantity rich white chocolate buttercream (see p23)

½ quantity royal icing (see p24)

TO DECORATE

2 x 250g packs ready to roll blue icing by Sainsbury's, kneaded together

500g pack ready to roll white icing by Sainsbury's

Icing sugar, for dusting

40g each ready to roll yellow, green, pink and fuchsia pink icings

9 strawberry laces by Sainsbury's

YOU WILL ALSO NEED

12 paper petits fours cases

1 large rectangular cake board

4cm round cutter

1 disposal piping bag

1 writing piping nozzle

1 small star-shaped piping nozzle

PER SERVING
598 cals, 23.3g fat, 13g sat fat, 79.7g total sugars, 0.23g salt

1 Preheat the oven to 180°C, fan 160°C, gas 4. Line a 22cm x 32cm x 5cm deep rectangular tin with baking paper (see p20). Place a petits fours case in each hole of a 12-hole mini muffin tray. Take 100g of the sponge mix and divide between the petits fours cases. Spoon the rest of the mixture into the cake tin and gently level the surface. Bake the mini muffins for 15-20 mins and the large cake for 1 hour-1 hour 15 mins. Remove and cool on wire racks.

2 Place the cake on the board and, if necessary, level the top with a serrated knife (see p21). Halve the cake horizontally and sandwich back together with half the buttercream. Reserve 2 tbsp of the buttercream and spread the rest in a thin and even layer over the top and sides of the cake.

3 Reserve 40g each of the blue and white icings. Knead half of the remaining white icing into the blue icing to give a pale blue colour, then knead in the rest of the white icing, just enough to form a marbled effect (picture A).

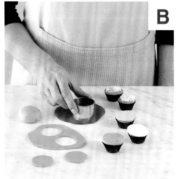
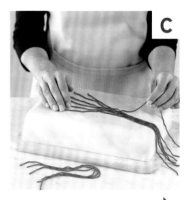

TURN OVER FOR THE REMAINING RECIPE STEPS ▶

Congratulations cake (continued)

4 Dust a surface with icing sugar and roll out the pale blue icing to a rectangle roughly 30cm x 42cm x 4mm thick. Use a rolling pin to drape the icing over the cake, then smooth down to make an even surface. Use a cake smoother, lightly dusted with icing sugar to give the icing a very smooth finish, moving it in a circular motion all over the cake. Trim the excess icing from around the base of the cake with a sharp knife.

5 Roll out the reserved blue and white icings and all the other coloured icings to 2mm thick. Using a 4cm round cutter stamp out 12 circles (2 from each colour). Spread the reserved 2 tbsp buttercream over the top of the mini muffins and top each one with a circle of coloured icing (picture B).

6 Arrange the strawberry laces as balloon strings across the cake, bringing them all together at the opposite side of the cake (picture C). Use a little of the royal icing to attach 9 of the mini muffins to the top of the cake over the strings (picture D).

7 Spoon half of the remaining royal icing into a piping bag fitted with the writing nozzle and pipe the word 'Congratulations' onto the main cake. Then pipe highlights onto the balloons (picture E).

8 Spoon the rest of the royal icing into the piping bag fitted with a small star-shaped nozzle. Pipe a shell border all around the base of the cake (picture F). Leave in a cool dry place until the royal icing has set. Serve the cake with the rest of the mini muffin balloons around it.

D

E

F

Cake variation

You can personalise this cake or change it to a birthday cake by adding candles and then piping the name and age (if you dare!) of the person onto the balloons.

New home cake

Give a warm welcome to a new home owner with this easy-to-make cake

RATING

SERVES 24

YOU WILL NEED
1 quantity chocolate sponge mixture baked in 2 x 20cm round cake tins for 45 mins (see p16), cooled

1/2 quantity vanilla buttercream (see p22)

TO DECORATE
Icing sugar, for dusting

120g ready to roll blue icing

2 x 500g packs ready to roll ivory icing by Sainsbury's, kneaded together

2 x 250g packs ready to roll green icing by Sainsbury's

60g ready to roll pink icing

60g ready to roll chocolate flavour icing

20g chocolate beans by Sainsbury's

50g ready to roll red icing

1 tbsp chocolate squares (from 142g pot chocolate sprinkles by Sainsbury's)

YOU WILL ALSO NEED
1 medium round board

Mini alphabet cutters

Triangle cutter (from mini cookie cutter set by Sainsbury's)

1 fine paint brush

PER SERVING
510 cals, 19.9g fat, 10.4g sat fat, 68.1g total sugars, 0.25g salt

1 Dust a surface with icing sugar. Knead 60g blue icing into 120g ivory icing until you have an even light blue colour. Shape into a rectangular block about 4cm x 4cm x 5cm. Set aside to firm up (if possible, leave out overnight, uncovered).

2 If necessary, trim the tops of the cakes to level (see p21), then sandwich them together with an even layer of the buttercream. Spread the remaining buttercream over the top and sides of the layered cakes.

3 Dust a surface with icing sugar. Roll out the remaining ivory icing to 4mm thick. Use a rolling pin to drape the icing over the cake, then smooth down to cover the cake completely. Trim the edges of the icing, reserving the trimmings.

4 Roll out 1 pack of the green icing to 2mm thick. Brush the cake board with a little boiled cooled water, then cover with the icing and trim (picture A); wrap and reserve the trimmings. Put the iced cake on the covered board. Dust

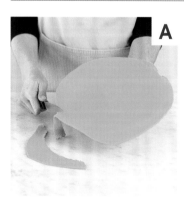
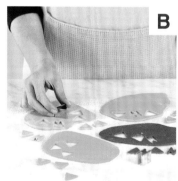
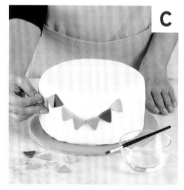

TURN OVER FOR THE REMAINING RECIPE STEPS

New home cake (continued)

a surface with icing sugar and roll out the remaining blue, the pink icing, 60g green icing and the chocolate icing to 2mm thick. Cut out letters in various colours to spell out 'new home' and set aside, then cut out 8 mini triangles from each icing (picture B). Using a little cooled boiled water, stick onto the cake side, all the way around, creating colourful bunting (picture C). Wrap and reserve the trimmings. Push a yellow chocolate bean into the peaks of the bunting.

5 Make the house decoration: dust a surface with icing sugar, roll out 25g ivory icing (from the reserved icing trimmings) to 1mm thick and cut out 4 x 1cm x 1.5cm squares for windows and 1 x 1cm x 2cm rectangle for a door. Using a little boiled water, stick them to the front of the blue icing rectangular block. Use the tip of a knife to make details on the door and windows. Push a yellow chocolate bean into the door for a handle. Shape the red icing into a 2cm x 4cm x 5cm block, then use a palette knife to press down two of the corners to make a roof shape (picture D). Gently press onto the house to secure and use a knife to make a tile pattern.

6 Roll out the remaining green icing to 2mm thick. Cut out a rough 8cm circle, place onto the top of the cake to one side, brush with a little water and place the house on top. To make the path, cut a 12cm x 2.5cm strip from the rolled out green icing, then create an impression in the middle of the strip with the handle of a wooden spoon (picture E). Brush the cake with a little cooled boiled water where you want the path to go and attach it; trim it to fit if necessary. Scatter the chocolate squares along the path.

7 Place the remaining chocolate beans around the bottom edge of the cake to create a neat finish.

8 Create the moving boxes by kneading together 10g chocolate icing and 50g ivory icing (from the remaining icing trimmings) to make an even light brown colour. Mould into 6 small cubes of varying sizes and create details using the tip of a knife. For open boxes, lay a small rectangular piece of icing over the top of the cube, make a small dent in the top with the end of a wooden spoon (picture F) and score the edges with a knife. Brush with cooled boiled water and top with small bits of rolled ivory icing to make 'polystyrene-style' packaging. Brush the bases of the boxes with cooled boiled water, then arrange them on the cake.

9 Finally, stick the 'new home' letters onto the cake with a little cooled boiled water.

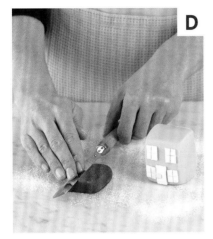

D

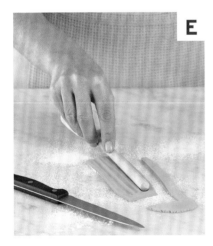

E

F

A fireside story...

The term 'housewarming' harks back to the days before central heating, when friends and family would bring around firewood as a welcoming gift to a new home owner. On top of keeping everyone nice and toasty, the fires were also said to cleanse the premises and ward off any evil spirits.

Garden lover's cake

A beautiful and inventive cake to warm the heart of any garden lover

RATING

SERVES 28

YOU WILL NEED
1 quantity rich white chocolate buttercream (see p23)

1¹/₂ quantities chocolate sponge mixture: 250g spooned into 2 tulip muffin cases by Sainsbury's and baked for 30 mins, cooled; the rest spread into 2 x 23cm round cake tins and baked for 45-50 mins (see p16), cooled

TO DECORATE
Icing sugar, for dusting

500g pack ready to roll soft chocolate flavour icing by Sainsbury's

2 tbsp apricot glaze by Sainsbury's, warmed

4 x 250g packs ready to roll green icing by Sainsbury's, kneaded together

6 chocolate fairy cakes by Sainsbury's, whizzed in a food processor

2 x 167g packs chocolate crunchy orange sticks by Sainsbury's

1 pack wild rose cake decorations by Sainsbury's

A few drops of green food colouring

100g ready to roll pink icing

¹/₂ pack mini blossom cake decorations by Sainsbury's

100g ready to roll white icing

Black, green and red writing icing pens (from 76g pack colour writing icing by Sainsbury's)

YOU WILL ALSO NEED
23cm round cake board

25cm square cake board

9 cocktail sticks

1 fine paint brush

4.5cm flower cutter

5cm round cutter

PER SERVING
797 cals, 32.8g fat, 17.1g sat fat, 104.8g total sugars, 0.36g salt

1 Use a couple of tablespoons of the buttercream to secure 1 x 23cm round cake onto the 23cm round cake board. Trim the top of the cake, if necessary (see p21), then spread half of the remaining buttercream over the top. Trim the top of the other cake, if necessary (see p21), then place upside down (to give a flat surface) on top of the first cake. Spread the remaining buttercream evenly up the sides and over the top. Chill while you prepare the square cake board.

2 Dust a surface with icing sugar and roll out the chocolate icing to 3mm thick. Brush the square cake board with a little apricot glaze, then use a rolling pin to drape the icing over the cake board (picture A). Smooth down with the palms of your hands for an even surface. Trim to fit the board.

3 Roll the green icing out to 4mm thick. Use a rolling pin to drape the icing over the round cake, then smooth with the palms of your hands to make an even surface. Trim the edges of the icing carefully using a small sharp knife.

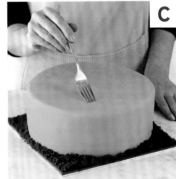

TURN OVER FOR THE REMAINING RECIPE STEPS

Garden lover's cake (continued)

4 Place the round cake on its cake board onto the centre of the brown iced square board. Brush the exposed brown icing around the round cake with glaze and sprinkle over two-thirds of the whizzed up chocolate fairy cakes to resemble soil, pressing down a little (picture B).

5 Using the back of a fork, prick and press the top of the cake all over to give the 'grass' some texture (picture C).

6 For the fence, brush 18 crunchy orange sticks with apricot glaze and stick to the sides of the cake at 2.5cm intervals. Cut the remaining orange sticks into halves and use to make the crossbars of the fence (picture D).

7 For the flower pots, brush the top of the baked chocolate muffins with glaze and sprinkle over most of the remaining whizzed up chocolate fairy cake crumbs to resemble soil. For one of the flower pots, top with the wild rose decorations. For the other, take 8 cocktail sticks and dip some kitchen paper in a little green food colouring and wipe over the sticks to make them look like green flower stalks. For the flowers, roll out the pink icing to 4mm thick, and use a 4.5cm flower cutter to cut out 4 flowers. Reserve the icing trimmings. Then stick a white mini blossom cake decoration in the middle of each flower using a dab of glaze. Repeat with the white icing and pink mini blossoms, reserving the icing trimmings.

Carefully push a cocktail stick into each flower (picture E) and then push into the flowerpot to make the flowers look like they are growing from the pot. Place the flower pots beside each other towards the back of the cake, securing with a little glaze.

8 For the seed packets, roll out the leftover pink and white icing to 4mm thick and from each one cut a 10cm x 7cm rectangle freehand, then a 5cm circle using a cutter. Use a cocktail stick to press in little marks at either end to look like sealed packets and 2 lines running horizontally just below and above the seal marks (picture F). With a little water, stick the opposite colour circles in the centre of each rectangle (white circle on pink rectangle and vice versa) to look like labels on the packets.

9 Using the black writing colour from the colour writing icing pack, write 'SEEDS' at the top of each packet. Draw flowers in one circle and a tomato in the other using the red and green writing icing from the pack.

10 Using a little glaze, secure the seed packets on top of the cake, one slightly up against a flower pot. Brush a little glaze around the base of the flower pot and sprinkle over the remaining chocolate fairy cake 'soil' crumbs.

11 Scatter the remaining mini blossoms around the bottom of the cake on top of the 'soil'.

D

E

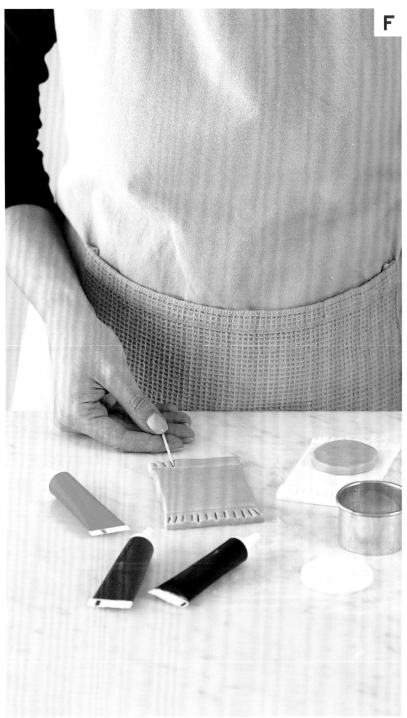

F

Try this
Why not decorate the cake as a vegetable patch like that of Beatrix Potter's infamous character Mr McGregor by completely covering it in fairy cake 'soil'. Then make or buy marzipan vegetables and fruits to arrange on the top.

Golf lover's cake

What could be better than a hole in one? This delightful golf-inspired cake, of course!

RATING 🧁🧁🧁

SERVES 32

YOU WILL NEED
1¹/₂ quantities quick chocolate buttercream (see p23)

2 quantities Victoria sponge mixture (see p14): three-quarters spread into 2 x 23cm round deep cake tins and baked for 1 hour, cooled; the remainder spread into 1 x 15cm round deep cake tin and baked for 30-40 mins, cooled

TO DECORATE
Icing sugar, for dusting

1.5kg ready to roll green icing, kneaded together

40g ready to roll black icing

60g ready to roll red icing (for the golf accessories, see p35 for more details)

50g ready to roll white icing (for the golf accessories, see p35 for more details)

2-3 tsp Taste the Difference cinnamon infused sugar

2 tbsp white caster sugar

1 tsp blue food colouring

YOU WILL ALSO NEED
1 large round cake plate

¹/₂ 1 cake pop stick by Sainsbury's, cut in half

1 cocktail stick

Small nail scissors

70cm x 1cm tartan ribbon

Double sided sticky tape

PER SERVING
671 cals, 28.3g fat, 16g sat fat, 87.3g total sugars, 0.25g salt

1 Spread a little chocolate buttercream on the cake plate and place one of the 23cm round cakes in the centre. Spread the top of the cake with chocolate buttercream and sandwich the other 23cm cake on top. Spread a little chocolate buttercream on the base of the 15cm cake and position on top of the other cakes, to one side. Push down lightly to secure.

2 Make the bunkers and water hazard. Using a small knife, carefully cut a shallow oval shape about 8cm long from one side of the top cake. Repeat on the 23cm cake to create another, then cut a kidney shape from the 23cm cake for the water hazard (picture A).

3 Take the pieces of sponge you removed, apply a little buttercream to the flat sides. Stick one on the 15cm cake to create an elevated green and the others on the 23cm cake to create a contoured fairway (picture B).

4 Using the remaining buttercream, cover the sides and tops of the cakes, including the mounds and dips. Don't worry if it looks a bit

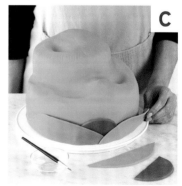

TURN OVER FOR THE REMAINING RECIPE STEPS ▶

Golf lover's cake (continued)

messy and uneven – the green icing will cover everything. Transfer to the fridge to chill for 45 mins, then use your fingertips to smooth out the buttercream and create more rounded contours for the bunkers and mounds.

5 Dust a surface with icing sugar and roll out the green icing to 4mm thick. Use a rolling pin to drape the icing over the stacked cakes. Using your fingertips, carefully smooth over the top of the cakes and into the bunkers; smooth down the sides of the cake with the palms of your hands. Trim the excess icing from the base of the cake with a small sharp knife and reserve the trimmings.

6 Press the back of a fork into the top and sides of each cake to create a grass-like texture.

7 Set aside 200g of the green icing trimmings. Take another 200g of trimmings and knead in 10g of the black icing to give a darker green. Repeat with another 200g of the green icing trimmings and 25g of the black icing. You will now have three shades of green.

8 To make the rolling hills for the larger cake, roll out the pure green icing to 3mm thick. Working freehand, cut out 2 x 18cm x 12cm eye shapes, then cut these in half widthways. Roll out the other 2 colours and cut a 14cm circle (using a small saucer as a guide) from one and a 10cm circle from another. Cut each of these in half. Using a little water, stick the semi-circles and hills onto the sides of the larger cake (picture C). Repeat to decorate the smaller cake, cutting out and halving 1 x 10cm circle, 1 x 12cm x 6cm eye shape and 1 x 10cm x 5cm eye shape.

9 To make a putting green, roll out a 12cm kidney bean shape from the mid-green icing. Stick it

on top of the mound on the small cake using a little water.

10 To make the golf bag, turn to p35. To make the flag, roll out the red icing and cut out a 5cm x 5cm x 4cm triangle. Attach the shorter side to the end of the halved pop stick by wrapping around the end of the stick and sealing with a little water. To create waves in the flag, drape it over a cocktail stick and leave to dry (picture D). For the number, roll out a little white icing, shape into a 6 and stick to the flag with a little water. Make a hole for the putting green with a small flattened ball of black icing, place on the cake and push the flag into the cake. Secure the golf bag next to the flag using a little water. Make golf balls with small balls of white icing and secure with a little water, too.

11 For the sand in the bunkers, brush the inside of the carved out areas (one on top of the 15cm and one on the 23cm cake) with water and sprinkle with the cinnamon infused sugar.

12 For the fir trees, take any one of the shades of green icing and roll a small piece into a cone. Starting at the base and working all the way up, make little cuts into the icing with small scissors (picture E). Repeat three more times using different shades of green and fix on the cakes with a little water. For instructions, turn to p35.

13 For the water hazard, put the caster sugar in a microwaveable bowl with 1 tbsp water and heat for 1 min 30 secs on high. Stir through the blue food colouring and, working quickly, spoon into the kidney-shaped hollow (picture F).

14 Wrap the ribbon around the base of the cake and secure the ends with double sided tape.

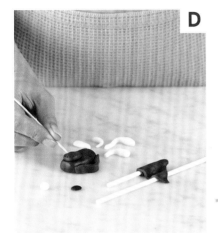

D

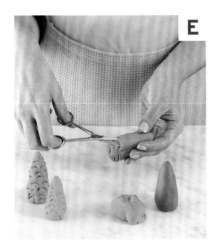

E

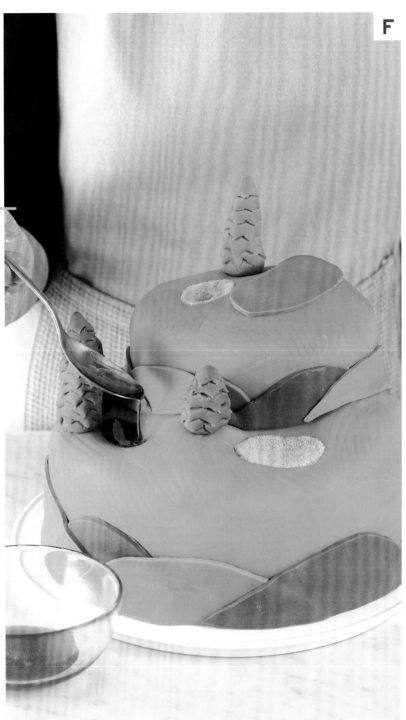

F

Golf lessons

The modern game of golf has its origins in Scotland. It's first mentioned in 15th century chronicles as being banned by King James II because it was proving an unwelcome distraction to the male populace, who should have been learning more useful skills such as archery!

Rainbow cake

Sunny skies and a colourful rainbow will brighten up any birthday party

RATING 🧁

SERVES 16

YOU WILL NEED
1 quantity Victoria sponge
mixture baked in 2 x 15cm
deep round cake tins for
40-45 mins (see p14),
cooled

1/2 quantity cream cheese
frosting (see p24)

1 quantity glacé icing
(see p22)

TO DECORATE
250g pack ready to
roll blue icing by
Sainsbury's

125g ready to roll
white icing

Icing sugar, for dusting

8-10 x 38g packs Smarties

250g pack ready to roll
yellow icing by Sainsbury's

50g white mini
marshmallows by
Sainsbury's, halved

YOU WILL ALSO NEED
1 medium cake plate

1 fine paint brush

6cm round cutter

PER SERVING
609 cals, 27.8g fat,
15.7g sat fat, 70.8g total
sugars, 0.3g salt

1 Put one of the cakes on a cake plate. Spread the top with frosting and sandwich the other cake on top. Spread one-third of the remaining frosting over the top and the sides of the cake, then spoon the rest onto the top of the cake to create a slight dome. Chill for 15 mins.

2 Twist the blue icing together with the white icing to create a marbled look. This will be used for the sky base. Dust a surface with icing sugar and roll out the icing to 4mm thick. Use a rolling pin to drape the icing over the cake, then smooth down to make an even surface. Trim the edges.

3 To make the rainbow, separate the Smarties into the different colours and put each colour into a bowl. You will need red, orange, yellow, green, blue and purple (the rest can be eaten or kept as a treat for another time!). Brush one side of each Smartie with a little glacé icing and stick onto the front section of the cake in curved rows, using a different colour for each row (picture A).

4 Dust a surface with icing sugar and roll out the yellow icing to 3mm thick. Cut 4 x 6cm round circles from the icing with the cutter. Using the edge of the cutter, shape 4 thin ovals for the sun's rays from 3 of the circles (picture B). Brush the back of the circle and the rays with the glacé icing, then stick them on the cake to make a sun.

5 Stick halved mini marshmallows grouped together onto the cake with a little glacé icing to make the shape of clouds (picture C).

A

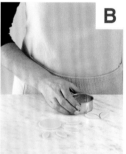
B

C

Piano cake

This showstopping creation is the perfect accompaniment to any musical celebration

RATING 🧁🧁🧁

SERVES 32

YOU WILL NEED
2 quantities Victoria sponge mixture baked in 2 x 20cm deep round cake tins for 1 hour (see p14), cooled

1 quantity rich white chocolate buttercream (see p23)

1/2 quantity royal icing (see p24)

TO DECORATE
Icing sugar, for dusting

250g pack ready to roll black icing by Sainsbury's

1kg pack ready to roll white icing by Sainsbury's

YOU WILL ALSO NEED
Cocktail sticks

25cm cake plate or board

1 disposable piping bag

1 small round writing piping nozzle

PER SERVING
594 cals, 25.2g fat, 14.3g sat fat, 74.1g total sugars, 0.23g salt

1 Make the decorations for the side and top of the cake. On a surface dusted with icing sugar, use your fingers to roll and flatten 75g of the black icing into musical notes and symbols (picture A), transferring to a sheet of baking paper as you go. Slide the baking paper onto a tray and set aside in a cool, dry place for 3-4 hours or overnight, until firm.

2 Trim the cakes, if necessary (see p21), then cut each one in half horizontally and sandwich the halves back together using 6 tbsp of the buttercream. Transfer to the freezer for 30 mins until quite firm.

3 Take the cakes out of the freezer. Place one on a chopping board, spread 4 tbsp buttercream over the top, then stack the second cake on top. Cut out the 3 piano cake templates on p190 from baking paper. Place the circular template number 1 on the top of the cake, to one side of it, then use cocktail sticks to mark the outline of the circle. Next, wrap template number 2 around the side of the cake, lining up

TURN OVER FOR THE REMAINING RECIPE STEPS ▶

Piano cake (continued)

the flat end of the triangle with the first cocktail stick of the circle on top of the cake. Use more cocktail sticks to mark a spiral along the edge of template 2 down the side of the cake, until you reach the other side of the circle at the bottom of the cake.

4 Using a serrated knife and following the line of the cocktail sticks, carve out a spiral from the top to the base of the cake, moving the board as you carve a section at a time (pictures B and C). The leftover sponge can be a cook's treat. Remove the cocktail sticks and return the cake to the freezer for 30 mins.

5 Remove the cake from the freezer. Spread the remaining buttercream in a thin layer all over the cake. Transfer the cake to the fridge and chill for 30 mins.

6 Remove the cake from the fridge and place on the cake plate. On a surface lightly dusted with icing sugar, roll out half the white icing to a large rectangle, roughly 16cm x 50cm x 5mm thick. Use templates 2 and 3 to cut out two shapes from the icing. Stick on the icing shape cut from template 2, starting at the tallest part of the cake and winding the icing triangle around the outside of the cake, down the spiral to the base (picture D). Attach the icing triangle cut from template 3 in the opposite direction, starting at the tallest part of the cake to join up with the other icing triangle, and winding it up the inner part of the spiral to the top of the cake. The ends of the two icing shapes may overlap a little – if so, trim them so they join

neatly. Trim the sides of the triangles, too, if necessary, then smooth the icing down with the palms of your hands.

7 Knead together the trimmings with 225g more white icing and roll out to a thickness of 5mm, then cut a circle from the icing using template number 1. Place on the top of the cake, smoothing it down with the palms of your hands (picture E).

8 For the keyboard, roll out 150g of the remaining soft white icing to a long strip roughly 7cm x 40cm x 5mm thick. Place on the flat surface of the spiral, trimming the edges with a sharp knife and smoothing with your hands. Score lightly with a knife to mark the piano keys.

9 Spoon the royal icing into a piping bag and snip off the end. Roll 25g of the remaining black icing out to 1mm-2mm thick and cut out 14 black piano keys. Attach in groups of two and three to the white keys, using some of the royal icing piped from the bag (picture F). Roll the rest of the black icing into a long thin strip about 3mm thick. Using a piece of kitchen string, measure around the top of the cake, the base of the cake and the edge of the spiral keyboard (picture G), then cut 3 x 1cm strips of black icing to these measurements. Attach the strips to the cake with royal icing piped from the bag (picture H).

10 Pipe dots of icing onto the backs of the notes and musical symbols, then press them gently onto the sides and top of the cake to finish.

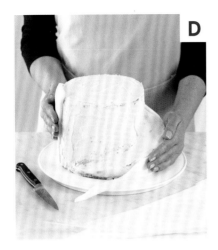

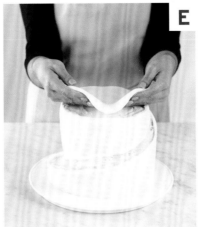

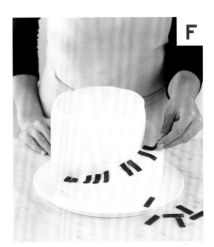

A winning formula

Alternatively, decorate this shaped cake as a race track by icing the sides and top of the cake in green icing and use black icing for the surface of the spiral to make the road. Make a car out of coloured marzipan and place it at the top of the spiral track.

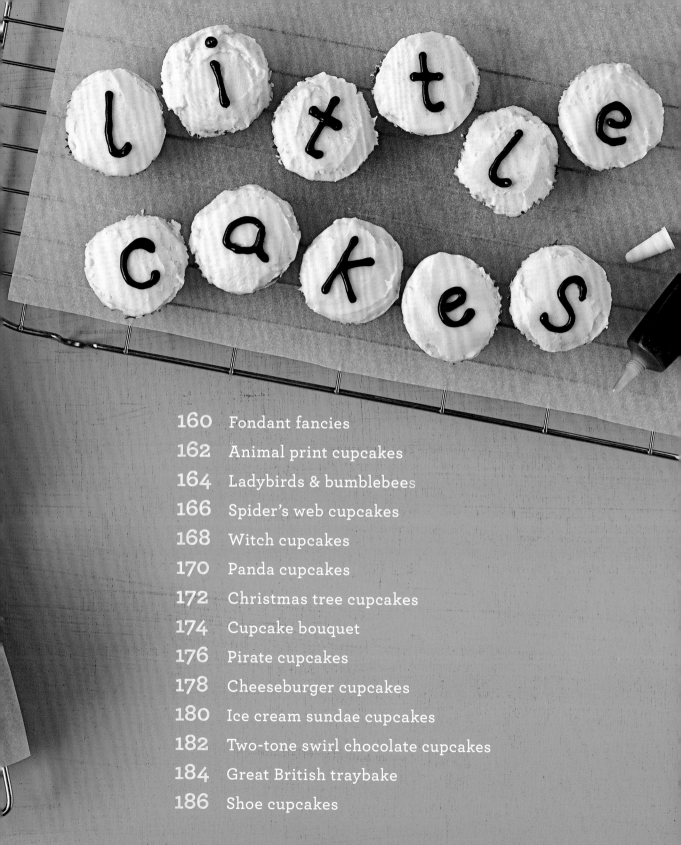

little cakes

Fondant fancies

Delicious iced sponge squares with a buttercream surprise – easy to make for a teatime treat

RATING

MAKES 25

YOU WILL NEED
1 quantity Victoria sponge mixture, flavoured with lemon, and baked in a 20cm square cake tin for 40-45 mins (see p14), cooled

1/2 quantity vanilla buttercream (see p22), with 2 tsp hot water beaten in

TO DECORATE
4 tbsp apricot glaze by Sainsbury's, warmed

Icing sugar, for dusting

250g white marzipan

2 x 500g packs fondant icing sugar

1/4 tsp each blue and pink food colouring

80g dark chocolate, melted and slightly cooled (see p25)

YOU WILL ALSO NEED
2 disposable piping bags

1 large round piping nozzle

12 cupcake cases (we used floral cupcake cases by Sainsbury's, in pink and blue)

PER CAKE
471 cals, 16.2g fat, 8.5g sat fat, 69.5g total sugars, 0.14g salt

1 Level the top of the cake with a serrated knife (see p21) and brush with the apricot glaze.

2 Dust a surface with icing sugar and roll out the marzipan to 3mm thick. Cut to the size of the cake, then use to cover the top. Chill in the fridge for 10 mins to firm up slightly.

3 Using a serrated knife, cut the cake into 25 x 4cm x 4cm squares (picture A): it's easiest to score the top lightly into a 5-column grid first. Spread some of the buttercream thinly over the sides of each square. Spoon the remaining buttercream into a piping bag and pipe a small blob on top of each square (picture B). Chill for 30 mins.

4 Meanwhile, make the fondant icing. Sift each pack of fondant icing sugar into 2 separate bowls. Gradually add about 90ml water to each bowl, stirring until the icing is a smooth paste. Colour one bowl with the blue colouring and the other with the pink, adding a few drops more if you want a stronger colour.

5 Spread the cakes out on a wire rack over a foil-lined baking tray, and use a spoon to carefully pour over the fondant icing, making sure it runs all the way down the sides to cover (picture C). Leave to set for 10-15 mins, then repeat and leave for 10-15 mins more.

6 Pour the melted chocolate into a piping bag and let it cool slightly. Snip off the very end of the bag and drizzle a thin chocolate zigzag over the tops of the cakes, then put into the cupcake cases, pinch the corners and serve.

Animal print cupcakes

Perfect for a child's themed party, and great fun to make for a roaring good time!

RATING

MAKES 12

YOU WILL NEED
1/2 quantity Victoria sponge mixture baked in 12 gold foil cupcake cases for 25 mins (see p14), cooled

TO DECORATE
Icing sugar, for dusting

250g ready to roll soft white icing

125g ready to roll yellow icing

1 tbsp apricot glaze by Sainsbury's, warmed

4 tsp black food colouring

YOU WILL ALSO NEED
6cm round cutter

1 fine paint brush

PER CAKE
308 cals, 12g fat, 6.6g sat fat, 38.2g total sugars, 0.14g salt

1 Using a serrated knife, slice the tops off the cupcakes to make them flat (see p21; picture A). You or the kids can eat the offcuts!

2 Dust a surface with icing sugar, then roll out the white icing to 3mm thick and, using a 6cm cutter, stamp out 8 circles. Repeat with the yellow icing, cutting out 4 circles (picture B). You may need to re-roll the trimmings to get enough circles.

3 Brush the cakes with warm apricot glaze and place an icing circle onto the top of each one, smoothing it to stick.

4 Using a small paint brush and the black food colouring, paint tiger stripes onto 4 yellow iced cakes, zebra stripes onto 4 of the white iced cakes, and a snow leopard print onto the other 4 white iced cakes (picture C). To get the grey colouring to fill in the leopard's spots, dilute the black food colouring with a little water.

Ladybirds & bumblebees

Perfect for a springtime tea party, these cute and colourful bugs are so easy to put together

RATING

MAKES 12

YOU WILL NEED
1/4 quantity rich white chocolate buttercream (see p23)

1/2 quantity Victoria sponge mixture baked in 12 brown paper cupcake cases for 25 mins (see p14), cooled

TO DECORATE

FOR THE LADYBIRDS
Icing sugar, for dusting

125g ready to roll red icing

75g ready to roll black icing

Black writing icing pen (from 76g pack colour writing icing by Sainsbury's)

12 white chocolate chips

FOR THE BUMBLEBEES
125g ready to roll yellow icing

1 liquorice Catherine wheel, unrolled

12 white chocolate chips

12 flaked almonds (replace with white chocolate buttons if serving to children under five)

1/4 tsp silver or gold edible lustre

YOU WILL ALSO NEED
6cm round cutter

1 fine paint brush

PER CAKE
408 cals, 18.1g fat, 10g sat fat, 49.6g total sugars, 0.15 salt

1 Using a serrated knife, slice the tops off the cupcakes to make them flat (see p21). For the ladybirds, dust a surface with icing sugar and roll out both the red and black icings to 3mm thick. Using a 6cm round cutter, stamp out 6 circles from the red icing and 3 from the black. Cut the black circles in half.

2 Spread a little buttercream onto 6 cakes and press the red circles on top (picture A). Press the black semi-circles on top of the red icing (to cover one half of the cakes), securing with a little writing icing. Then use the writing icing to add dots to the red bodies. Add 2 chocolate chips to each black head and add a dot of writing icing in the centre of each one for the eyes. Score down the centre of each visible red semi-circle with a knife to indicate the wings.

3 To make the bumblebees, dust a surface with icing sugar and roll out the yellow icing to 3mm thick. Using a 6cm round cutter, stamp out 6 circles. Spread a little buttercream onto the remaining 6 cakes and press the yellow circles on top, for the bodies.

4 Use the writing icing to make half-moon faces (picture B). Cut the liquorice into 6 x 6cm strips and 6 x 5cm strips. Pipe a little black writing icing onto each strip and press gently onto the bodies to make the stripes (picture C). Press 2 chocolate chips into each face and add a dot of the black writing icing in the centre of each one for eyes.

5 Using a fine paint brush, dust the flaked almonds with the lustre, then press into the bodies for wings.

Spider's web cupcakes

They're creepy, they're crawly, they're totally tasty. Bake a batch of these scary treats for Halloween

RATING

MAKES 12

YOU WILL NEED
1/2 quantity chocolate sponge mixture baked in 12 brown paper cupcake cases for 25 mins (see p16), cooled

TO DECORATE
3 tbsp orange juice

250g icing sugar

2 black writing icing pens (from 2 x 76g packs colour writing icing by Sainsbury's)

205g ready to roll black icing

20g ready to roll orange icing

YOU WILL ALSO NEED
1 skewer or cocktail stick

PER CAKE
408 cals, 13.9g fat, 6.8g sat fat, 57.4g total sugars, 0.25g salt

1   Trim the tops of the cakes to make a flat surface (see p21). Mix the orange juice with the icing sugar to get a thick, spreadable icing, you may need to add a few more drops of juice as you mix. Spread the orange icing over the cupcakes (picture A).

2   Starting from the centre of each cupcake to the outside, draw 4 ever larger circles on top of the icing with one of the black writing icing pens. Immediately (while still wet) drag a skewer (or cocktail stick) outwards from the middle to create a cobweb effect (picture B).

3   To make the spiders, take 80g of the black icing. Divide into 12 even-size pieces and roll into balls. Take 25g black icing and divide into 12 even-size pieces, then roll into balls. Stick the smaller balls for the head onto the bigger balls for the body, using a little water or writing icing to secure.

4   To make one spider's legs and eyes, roll out 4 x 2g pieces of black icing into thin 6cm sausage shapes. Roll out 2 tiny balls of orange icing to make the eyes.

5   To finish, line the legs up in a row and place the head and body of a spider on top, sticking with a little water or writing icing, if necessary. Use a cocktail stick to lift the legs into a slightly bent position (picture C). Stick the orange eyes onto the head of the spider and secure with writing icing. Dot writing icing in the middle of each eye to make pupils. Repeat to make legs and eyes for the remaining spiders. When the cupcake icing has set, put a spider on top of each one.

Witch cupcakes

Double, double, toil and trouble... Look who's crashed their broomstick into a pile of sweet buttercream!

RATING

MAKES 12

YOU WILL NEED
1 quantity vanilla
buttercream (see p22)

½ quantity Victoria
sponge mixture baked in
12 brown paper cupcake
cases for 25 mins (see
p14), cooled

TO DECORATE
Icing sugar, for dusting

2 x 250g packs ready
to roll black icing
by Sainsbury's

100g ready to roll
white icing

50g ready to roll red icing

60g ready to roll chocolate
flavoured icing

12 chocolate crunchy
mint sticks by
Sainsbury's

6 tsp chocolate vermicelli
by Sainsbury's

YOU WILL ALSO NEED
5cm round cutter

1 fine paint brush

1 disposable piping bag

1 large star-shaped
piping nozzle

PER CAKE
765 cals, 31.9g fat,
18.3g sat fat, 107.6g total
sugars, 0.16 salt

1 Dust a surface with icing sugar and roll out
1 pack black icing to 3mm thick. Cut into 12 x
5cm rounds for the rims of the hats. Set aside.

2 Set aside 55g from the remaining pack of black
icing for the legs and broomsticks. Divide the
rest of the pack into 12 x 15g pieces and use
to mould into cone shapes for the tops of the
witches' hats. Brush the bottom with a little
water and stick onto the circles (picture A).

3 To create the witches' legs, roll 2 x 20g pieces
of both the white and black icings separately to
form 4 x 1cm x 30cm strips. Place next to each
other, alternating the colours, stick together
with a little water, then cut 1cm pieces along
the length, and roll each one into a sausage
shape to make black and white legs (picture B).
You will need 24 in all. Mould the red icing into
shoes and attach with a little water to the legs.

4 To make the broomsticks, knead 25g white icing
with the chocolate icing to make a light brown
colour. Roll out to 2mm thick and cut into 2cm
x 5cm pieces. Cut bristles 1-2mm apart along
the 5cm strip, but only half way across the strip.
Roll the strip around one end of the mint stick to
make the broom (picture C). Roll out 15g black
icing to 2mm thick and cut into thin strips to
wrap around the end of the 'bristles'.

5 Spoon the buttercream into a piping bag fitted
with the star nozzle. Pipe a swirl onto each
cupcake, then put a hat onto one side of each
cupcake, with the legs on the other and the
broom to one side. Scatter over vermicelli.

Panda cupcakes

These appealing little cakes are super cute and will appeal to kids of all ages – as well as adults!

RATING

MAKES 12

YOU WILL NEED
1/2 quantity vanilla buttercream (see p22)

1/2 quantity Victoria sponge mixture baked in 12 silver foil paper cupcake cases for 25 mins (see p14), cooled

TO DECORATE
100g ready to roll black icing

2 tbsp desiccated coconut

24 white chocolate chips

1 black writing icing pen (from 76g pack colour writing icing by Sainsbury's)

YOU WILL ALSO NEED
2cm round cutter

1.5cm round cutter

1 fine paint brush

PER CAKE
399 cals, 20.6g fat, 11.9g sat fat, 42.4g total sugars, 0.15 g salt

1   Spread the buttercream over the cupcakes to make smooth domed tops.

2   Roll out the black icing to 3mm thick. Cut out 24 x 2cm circles for the ears and 24 x 1.5cm circles for the bases of the eyes. Using the remaining black icing, roll 12 balls, each about the size of a blueberry, for the noses of your pandas. Slightly curve the 2cm circles into ear shapes.

3   Press the noses and the bases of the eyes lightly onto the cupcakes, then sprinkle the desiccated coconut over the rest of the surfaces – it will stick to the buttercream (picture A). If any of the coconut stays on the eyes or noses, gently brush it away with the paint brush.

4   Press white chocolate chips into place for the eyeballs. Using the black writing icing pen, make pupils in the centres, then draw a mouth under each nose (picture B).

5   Finish the panda faces by making 2 small indentations with a knife where the ears will go, then gently pressing the black icing circles into them so that about a quarter of each is embedded in the sponges (picture C).

A

B

C

Christmas tree cupcakes

Everyone will love these festive cupcakes with a hidden surprise

RATING

MAKES 12

YOU WILL NEED
1¹/₂ quantities rich white chocolate buttercream (see p23)

¹/₂ quantity chocolate sponge mixture baked in 12 brown paper cupcake cases for 25 mins (see p16), cooled

TO DECORATE
100g dark chocolate, melted and cooled slightly (see p25)

5 tsp green food colouring

¹/₄ tsp black food colouring

12 small strawberries with the hull ends sliced off to make flat bases

2 tbsp gold pearls by Sainsbury's

2 tbsp silver balls by Sainsbury's

YOU WILL ALSO NEED
2 disposable piping bags

1 large star-shaped piping nozzle

PER CAKE
854 cals, 45.9g fat, 26.2g sat fat, 94.6g total sugars, 0.3g salt

1 Pour the melted chocolate into a disposable piping bag. Snip off the very tip of the bag and pipe little stars onto a sheet of baking paper (picture A). Slide the baking parchment onto a baking sheet and put into the fridge to set while you prepare the cupcakes.

2 Mix the buttercream with the green and black food colourings to get a deep, rich green. Spoon most of it into a second piping bag fitted with a star nozzle. (You may need to work in batches if the icing won't all fit in one go.)

3 Pipe a little buttercream onto each cupcake and top with an upended strawberry (picture B). Pipe the rest of the buttercream all over the strawberries to create a tree effect, with more stars at the bases, getting fewer towards the tips (picture C). Try to pipe larger stars at the bottom and slightly smaller ones as you get to the top. Decorate the cupcakes with the gold pearls, silver balls and the chocolate stars.

Cook's tip: To make a festive snowman figure similar to the one pictured, see p34.

A

B

C

Cupcake bouquet

A pretty bunch of cupcake 'flowers' makes a wonderful Mother's Day treat

RATING

MAKES 12

YOU WILL NEED
1 quantity rich white chocolate buttercream (see p23)

1/2 quantity Victoria sponge mixture baked in 12 brown paper cupcake cases for 25 mins, cooled (see p14)

TO DECORATE
2 tsp blue food colouring

1 tsp pink food colouring

YOU WILL ALSO NEED
3 disposable piping bags

1 small star-shaped piping nozzle

16cm dry foam sphere (available from florists)

16cm flower pot

4 long wooden skewers, each cut into thirds

30 squares green tissue paper (10cm x 10cm)

Cocktail sticks

PER CAKE
505 cals, 27.3g fat, 15.8g sat fat, 53.9g total sugars, 0.15g salt

1 Divide the buttercream in half and spoon into 2 bowls. Add 1 tsp blue colouring to one bowl, and the remaining blue colouring and the pink colouring to the other. Beat until the colour is completely combined, then spoon half of each icing into separate disposable piping bags.

2 Snip the ends off each, leaving a 1cm-2cm hole. Place both bags into a third piping bag, also with the end snipped off and fitted with a star-shaped piping nozzle (picture A). Make sure both inner bags are pushed all the way down towards the nozzle. Squeeze the icing bags from the top to move the buttercream down towards the nozzle so that both colours will come through to create a two-colour effect.

3 Starting from the outside, squeeze star shapes onto the top of the cakes (picture B). Continue in a spiral towards the centre of each one (picture B). You only want one layer, but all gaps should be filled. Refill the piping bags with the remaining icing when they run out.

4 Rest the foam sphere on the flower pot so the bottom half is inside the pot. Insert the 12 skewers, leaving 2.5cm-5cm gaps between them. Push the skewers into the foam sphere until only 3cm of the skewer is showing.

5 Press the cakes all the way down on the skewers (picture C). Wait until the buttercream has set, then scrunch up the squares of tissue paper, squeezing each one in from the middle. Place the tissue between the cupcakes, making sure the paper does not touch the cakes, and secure with cocktail sticks, if necessary.

Pirate cupcakes

Shiver me timbers, these are perfect for a children's party – or just some swashbuckling fun!

RATING

MAKES 12

YOU WILL NEED
1/2 quantity rich white chocolate buttercream (see p23)

1/2 quantity chocolate sponge mixture baked in 12 brown paper cupcake cases for 25 mins (see p16), cooled

TO DECORATE
1/4 tsp pink food colouring

Icing sugar, for dusting

250g pack ready to roll red icing by Sainsbury's

125g ready to roll black icing

12 white chocolate chips

12 blanched hazelnuts (replace with chocolate chips if serving to children under five)

1/2 x 69g pot chocolate vermicelli by Sainsbury's

1 black writing icing pen (from 76g pack colour writing icing pack by Sainsbury's)

YOU WILL ALSO NEED
6cm round cutter

PER CAKE
590 cals, 26.8g fat, 13.9g sat fat, 72.6g total sugars, 0.27g salt

1 Mix the pink food colouring into the buttercream to get a light pink colour.

2 Dust a surface with icing sugar and roll out the red icing to 3mm thick. Using the 6cm cutter, cut out 6 circles, then slice each one into 3. The outer rounded sections will become bandanas. Cut 24 small teardrop shapes from the middle sections to make the bandana ties (picture A).

3 Dust a surface with icing sugar and roll out the black icing to 3mm thick. Working freehand, cut out 12 x 1.5cm circles for the eyepatches and 24 teardrop shapes for moustaches. Slice 12 x 2mm wide lengths to make eyepatch strings (picture B) and cut to the width of the cakes.

4 Spread the buttercream over the top of the cupcakes. Stick a red bandana shape onto the top third of each cupcake and put 2 teardrop-shaped red ties on one side of each bandana, using a little water to help them stick. Underneath, place a white chocolate chip, pointed side down, as one eye. Next to that, stick a small black circle with the top cut off for the eyepatch. Put the eyepatch strings in place.

5 Create a nose with a hazelnut and stick 2 back-to-back black teardrop shapes underneath it for the moustache, curling the ends slightly. Finish each pirate with a sprinkle of the chocolate vermicelli for the beard (picture C) and use the writing icing to create spots on the bandanas and pupils on the chocolate chip eyes.

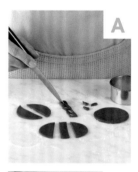

A

B

C

Cheeseburger cupcakes

Give everyone a surprise with these savoury favourites in deliciously layered cake form!

RATING

MAKES **9**

YOU WILL NEED
2 tbsp semi skimmed milk

1/2 quantity Victoria sponge mixture (see p14)

1 tbsp cocoa powder

1/2 quantity vanilla buttercream (see p22)

TO DECORATE
1 tsp apricot glaze by Sainsbury's

3 tsp white, orange and yellow sprinkles by Sainsbury's

Icing sugar, for dusting

100g ready to roll yellow icing

100g ready to roll green icing

Red writing icing pen (from 76g pack colour writing icing by Sainsbury's)

YOU WILL ALSO NEED
12 paper cupcake cases

6.5cm round cutter

1 cocktail stick

PER SERVING
562 cals, 26.8g fat, 15.2g sat fat, 65.2g total sugars, 0.23g salt

1 Preheat the oven to 180°C, fan 160°C, gas 4. Place the paper cupcake cases in a 12-hole muffin tin. Stir the milk into the Victoria sponge mixture, then divide three-quarters of it equally between 9 muffin cases. Stir the cocoa powder into the rest of the mixture, then spoon into the last 3 paper cases. Bake all the cakes for 25 mins. Cool on a wire rack.

2 Peel the paper cases off the cupcakes. Halve the Victoria sponge cakes horizontally for the burger buns and cut each of the chocolate muffins into 3 horizontally to make 9 burgers (picture A). Brush the domed tops of the Victoria muffin halves with apricot glaze, then scatter the coloured sprinkles over to resemble seeds.

3 Dust a surface with icing sugar and roll out the yellow and green icings to 3mm thick each. Using a 6.5cm round cutter, stamp out 9 circles from each colour.

4 Gently flatten the yellow icing circles around the edges with your fingers for the cheese and put to one side. Roll the end of a cocktail stick around the edges of the green circles to create a crinkled effect for the lettuce (picture B).

5 Spread the bottom halves of the Victoria sponges with a little buttercream and top with 'lettuce'. Add more buttercream and top with a 'burger', then more buttercream and a slice of 'cheese'. Pipe red 'ketchup' on each (picture C), using the writing icing pen, finish with the Victoria sponge 'bun' tops and serve.

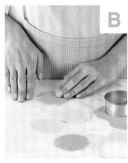

Ice cream sundae cupcakes

These tempting little cakes are gorgeous treats to enjoy with strawberry milk!

RATING 🧁

MAKES 12

YOU WILL NEED
3/4 quantity rich white chocolate buttercream (see p23)

1/2 quantity Victoria sponge mixture baked in 12 floral cupcake cases for 25 mins (see p14), cooled

1/4 quantity biscuit dough (see p19)

2/3 quantity chocolate ganache (made with 100ml double cream and 100g dark chocolate, see p22)

TO DECORATE
Plain flour, for dusting

Icing sugar, for dusting

125g ready to roll soft white icing

125g ready to roll fuchsia pink icing

12 glacé cherries

YOU WILL ALSO NEED
11cm round cutter

4cm or 5cm round cutter

1 disposable piping bag

1 small star-shaped piping nozzle

PER SERVING
726 cals, 37.2g fat, 21.8g sat fat, 76.4g total sugars, 0.17g salt

1 Spoon half of the buttercream onto the tops of the cupcakes, then use a palette knife to create a dome of buttercream on each one for the icing to rest on (picture A).

2 Preheat the oven to 190°C, fan 170°C, gas 5. Line a baking tray with baking paper. Dust a surface with a little flour and roll out the biscuit dough to 3mm thick. Cut out 3 x 11cm rounds, then cut each round into quarters to make 'wafer fans'. Place on the baking tray and mark a criss-cross pattern onto each with a knife (picture B). You will need to mark the dough relatively deeply, otherwise the markings will fade as the dough rises slightly when baking. Bake the biscuits for 8-10 mins, until golden at the edges. Remove and cool on a wire rack.

3 Dust a surface with icing sugar and separately roll out the white and fuchsia pink icings to 3mm thick. With the 4cm or 5cm round cutter, cut 6 circles each of white and pink icing.

4 Place a circle of white or pink icing onto each cupcake. Drizzle over the slightly cooled chocolate ganache, letting it spread across the icing (picture C). Put the remaining buttercream into a piping bag fitted with a star-shaped piping nozzle and pipe a small swirl on top of the ganache on each cupcake and top with a glacé cherry.

5 Cut a small incision into the top edge of each cupcake and insert a 'wafer fan' in each to finish.

Two-tone swirl chocolate cupcakes

Rich chocolate sponges topped with white and dark chocolate buttercream for the ultimate indulgence

RATING 🧁

MAKES 12

YOU WILL NEED
50g white chocolate chips

1/2 quantity chocolate sponge mixture (see p16)

1/2 quantity rich white chocolate buttercream (see p23)

1/2 quantity rich dark chocolate buttercream (see p23)

TO DECORATE
1 tbsp chocolate squares (from 142g pack chocolate sprinkles by Sainsbury's)

YOU WILL ALSO NEED
12 brown paper cupcake cases

3 disposable piping bags

1 large star-shaped piping nozzle

PER SERVING
632 cals, 34g fat, 19g sat fat, 67.1g total sugars, 0.28g salt

1 Preheat the oven to 180°C, fan 160°C, gas 4. Put the cupcake cases into a 12-hole muffin tin. Stir the white chocolate chips into the chocolate sponge mixture (picture A), then fill each of the cupcake cases two-thirds full with the mixture and bake for 25 mins. Cool completely on a wire rack.

2 Spoon each buttercream into separate piping bags (without nozzles), being careful not to overfill them. Snip the ends off each, leaving a 1cm-2cm hole. Snip the end off a third bag and fit it with a star nozzle, then put the two bags that are filled with icing into it (picture B). Make sure both inner bags are pushed all the way down towards the nozzle. Squeeze the icing bags from the top to move the buttercream down towards the nozzle, then pipe swirls onto your cupcakes for a two-tone effect (picture C).

3 Finish by sprinkling on the chocolate squares.

Great British traybake

Celebrate all things British and create these simple little sponges with a cheery patriotic twist

RATING

MAKES 9

YOU WILL NEED
1 quantity Victoria sponge mixture baked in a 32cm x 22cm x 5cm deep rectangular baking tray for 1 hour (see p14), cooled

¹⁄₄ quantity vanilla buttercream (see p22)

TO DECORATE
Icing sugar, for dusting

150g ready to roll soft ivory icing

150g ready to roll blue icing

100g ready to roll red icing

1 tbsp apricot glaze by Sainsbury's

2 tbsp blue & white sugar pearls from a 69g pot red, blue & white pearls by Sainsbury's

¹⁄₄ x 75g bag strawberry laces by Sainsbury's

PER SERVING
774 cals, 35.4g fat, 19.7g sat fat, 84g total sugars, 0.39g salt

1 If necessary, trim the cake to make a flat surface (see p21). Dust a surface with icing sugar and roll out the ivory icing to 3mm thick. Measure the top of the Victoria sponge and cut the ivory icing to the same size. Spoon the buttercream over the top of the cake and spread evenly to cover. Use a rolling pin to drape the ivory icing over the sponge (picture A), then smooth down all over to make an even surface. Trim the edges and discard any excess, then cut the cake into 9 even-sized rectangular pieces.

2 Dust a surface with icing sugar and roll out both the blue and red icings to 2mm thick. To make 6 Union Jacks: from the red icing, cut 6 x 1cm x 9.5cm strips and 6 x 1cm x 6.5cm strips for the crosses; from the blue icing, cut 6 x 8cm x 5cm rectangles; cut these into quarters, then cut each quarter into 2 triangles (picture B). Using apricot glaze, stick the red crosses to the ivory icing and fit 2 blue triangles in each corner to form a Union Jack design (picture C). To finish, place 16-18 blue or white sugar pearls along the centre of the red icing crosses.

3 To make 3 blue and red Union Jacks with red bows, cut 3 x 9cm x 6cm blue icing rectangles; cut these into quarters, then cut each quarter into 2 triangles. Stick to the ivory icing with apricot glaze. Using more apricot glaze, stick lengths of strawberry laces into the spaces between the blue triangles. Use more laces to create bows and attach these to the middle of the cakes with a little glaze.

A

B

C

Shoe cupcakes

These gorgeous high-heeled cupcakes are the perfect choice for fashionistas

RATING

MAKES 12

YOU WILL NEED
Plain flour, for dusting

¼ quantity biscuit dough mixture (see p19)

1 quantity vanilla buttercream (see p22)

½ quantity Victoria sponge mixture baked in 12 fairy cake paper cases by Sainsbury's in a muffin tray for 20 mins (see p14), cooled

12 chocolate wafer curls (Askey's Deluxe Café Curls)

TO DECORATE
250g white chocolate

1 tsp each cochineal red, yellow and green food colourings

2 tsp white shimmer pearls by Sainsbury's

4 white lustre roses by Sainsbury's

16 mini blossom cake decorations by Sainsbury's

2 tsp pink glimmer sugar by Sainsbury's

2 tbsp butterfly confetti by Sainsbury's

2 tbsp red confetti hearts by Sainsbury's

YOU WILL ALSO NEED
3 disposable piping bags

2 star-shaped piping nozzles and 1 small round piping nozzle

PER SERVING
734 cals, 39.6g fat, 23.4g sat fat, 72.5g total sugars, 0.24g salt

1 Preheat the oven to 190°C, fan 170°C, gas 5. Dust a surface with flour and roll out the biscuit dough to 3mm thick. Cut out 12 heel-shaped biscuits, using the template on p190 (picture A). Put the biscuits on a non-stick baking tray and bake for 10-12 mins, until golden at the edges. Remove and allow to cool.

2 Line a baking tray with baking paper. Melt 200g white chocolate in bowl set over a pan of simmering water (see p25 for more information). Dip each biscuit in the chocolate, leaving only 1cm uncovered at the end (picture B). Place the biscuits on the baking tray and put in the fridge until set.

3 Divide the buttercream equally between 3 small bowls. Add a different food colouring to each bowl and mix well until evenly coloured. Spoon each coloured buttercream into 3 separate disposable piping bags fitted with the nozzles. Pipe the different coloured buttercream and patterns onto the cakes.

4 Gently push the uncovered end of the white chocolate biscuits into the buttercream and slightly into the cake. To create the stiletto heels, melt the remaining 50g white chocolate as before, cut the wafer curls at an angle to make sure they sit flush against the biscuit shoe and your work surface, then attach to the undersides of the biscuits using the melted chocolate (picture C). Leave to set for 10 mins. Decorate each shoe cupcake with the different cake decorations, as desired.

Cake templates

These are all the templates you'll need to create the more complicated shapes in this book, coded by colour. Simply trace the shape you need onto baking paper

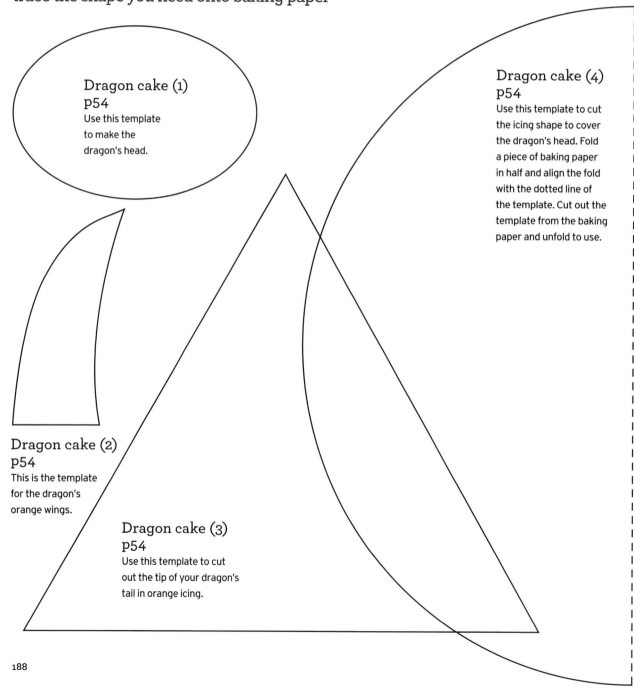

Dragon cake (1)
p54
Use this template
to make the
dragon's head.

Dragon cake (4)
p54
Use this template to cut
the icing shape to cover
the dragon's head. Fold
a piece of baking paper
in half and align the fold
with the dotted line of
the template. Cut out the
template from the baking
paper and unfold to use.

Dragon cake (2)
p54
This is the template
for the dragon's
orange wings.

Dragon cake (3)
p54
Use this template to cut
out the tip of your dragon's
tail in orange icing.

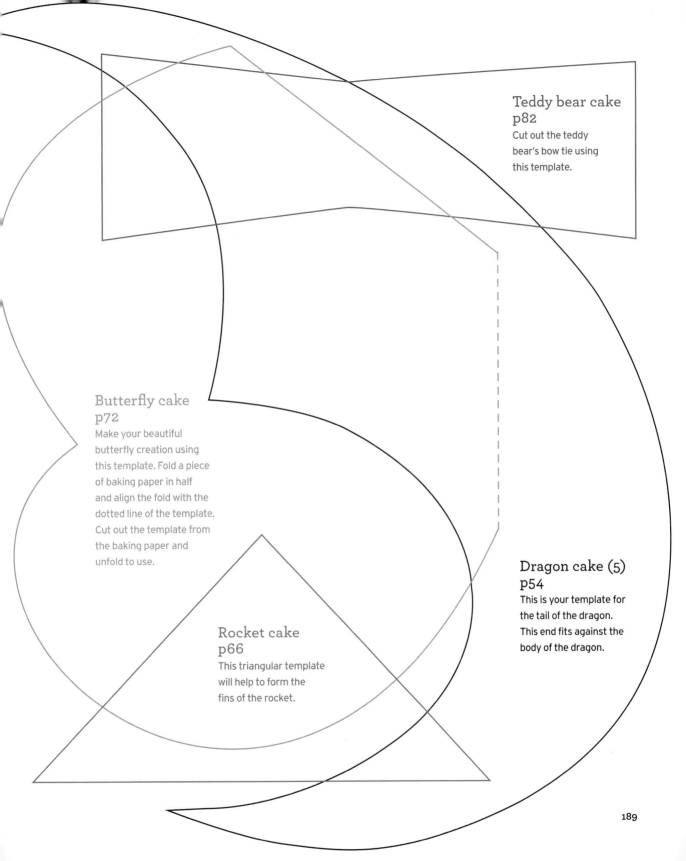

**Teddy bear cake
p82**
Cut out the teddy bear's bow tie using this template.

**Butterfly cake
p72**
Make your beautiful butterfly creation using this template. Fold a piece of baking paper in half and align the fold with the dotted line of the template. Cut out the template from the baking paper and unfold to use.

**Dragon cake (5)
p54**
This is your template for the tail of the dragon. This end fits against the body of the dragon.

**Rocket cake
p66**
This triangular template will help to form the fins of the rocket.

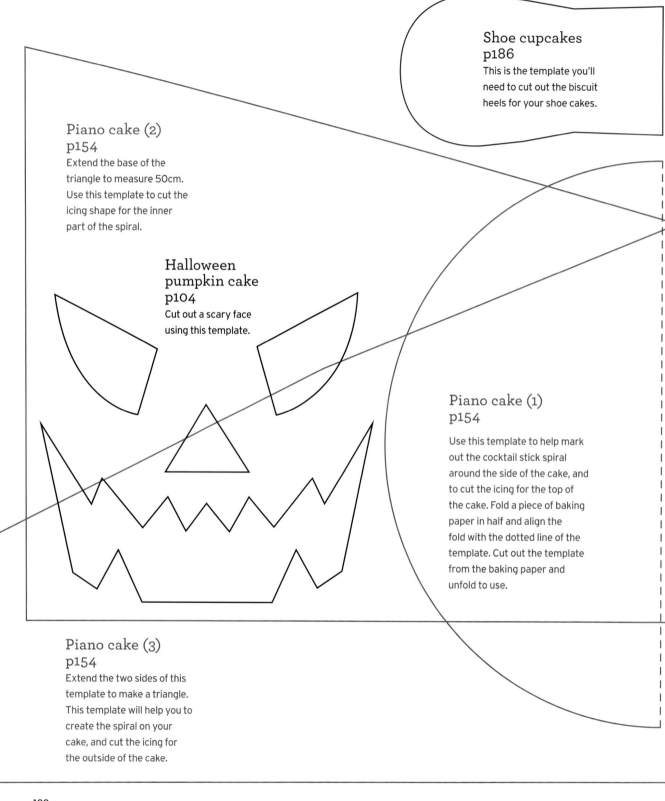

**Shoe cupcakes
p186**
This is the template you'll need to cut out the biscuit heels for your shoe cakes.

**Piano cake (2)
p154**
Extend the base of the triangle to measure 50cm. Use this template to cut the icing shape for the inner part of the spiral.

**Halloween pumpkin cake
p104**
Cut out a scary face using this template.

**Piano cake (1)
p154**

Use this template to help mark out the cocktail stick spiral around the side of the cake, and to cut the icing for the top of the cake. Fold a piece of baking paper in half and align the fold with the dotted line of the template. Cut out the template from the baking paper and unfold to use.

**Piano cake (3)
p154**
Extend the two sides of this template to make a triangle. This template will help you to create the spiral on your cake, and cut the icing for the outside of the cake.

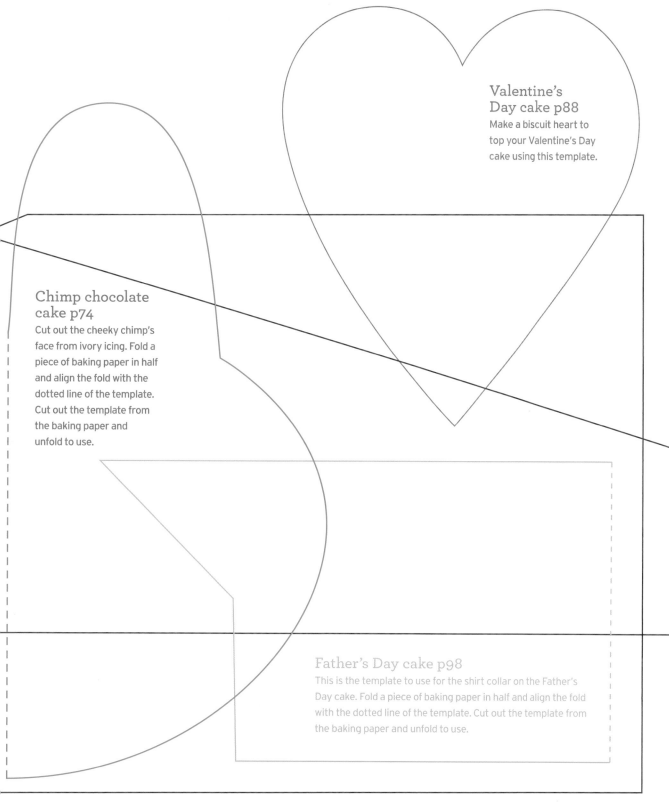

Valentine's
Day cake p88
Make a biscuit heart to
top your Valentine's Day
cake using this template.

Chimp chocolate
cake p74
Cut out the cheeky chimp's
face from ivory icing. Fold a
piece of baking paper in half
and align the fold with the
dotted line of the template.
Cut out the template from
the baking paper and
unfold to use.

Father's Day cake p98
This is the template to use for the shirt collar on the Father's
Day cake. Fold a piece of baking paper in half and align the fold
with the dotted line of the template. Cut out the template from
the baking paper and unfold to use.

All the cakes at a glance

This colourful collection of cakes includes something for all those big occasions, from birthdays and weddings to special days such as Christmas, Easter and Valentine's Day.

Animal print cupcakes 162

Bonfire cake 108

Bunny cake 42

Butterfly cake 72

Cheeseburger cupcakes 178

Chimp chocolate cake 74

Choo-choo train cake 62

Christmas house cake 114

Christmas tree cupcakes 172

Congratulations cake 136

Cupcake bouquet 174

Daisy wedding cake 120

Dragon cake 54

Easter chocolate cake 92

Fairy tale castle cake 58

Father's Day shirt & tie cake 98

Flower cake 40

Fondant fancies 160

Football shirt cake 70

Garden lover's cake 144

Gift box cake 130

Golf lover's cake 148

Great British traybake 184

Halloween graveyard cake 102

Halloween pumpkin cake 104

Happy anniversary cake 128

Ice cream sundae cupcakes 180

Kitty cat cake 80

Ladybirds & bumblebees 164

Little piggy cake 78

Mother's Day cake 94

New baby cake 134

New home cake 140

Panda cupcakes 170

Piano cake 154

Pirate cupcakes 176

Rainbow cake 152

Rocket cake 66

Ruffle wedding cake 124

Seaside cake 50

Sheep cake 76

Shoe cupcakes 186

Simple Christmas cake 112

Spider's web cupcakes 166

Surprise cake 46

Teddy bears' picnic cake 82

Treasure chest cake 44

Two-tone swirl chocolate cupcakes 182

Valentine's Day cake 88

Witch cupcakes 168

Index

To make the chocolate and vanilla traybake on p158, spread 1 quantity of chocolate sponge mixture (p16) into a 32cm x 22cm x 5cm deep rectangular baking tray and bake in a preheated oven at 180°C, fan 160°C, gas 4 oven for 1 hour. Remove from the oven and cool, then spread over 1 quantity of vanilla buttercream (p22) and sprinkle with desiccated coconut. Decorate with shapes cut from ready to roll chocolate flavour icing.

General safety tips
- Always wash your hands before baking. Wash fresh fruit before using.
- Keep children away from hot ovens, hobs and knives.
- Be aware of potential allergies, such as nut allergies, when making cakes for other people. Check packaging for any allergens.
- Public health advice is to avoid consumption of raw or lightly cooked eggs, especially those vulnerable to infection, including pregnant women, babies and the elderly.
- Please consider age suitability when serving cakes containing whole nuts to under fives (a potential choking hazard).
- Do not leave candles unattended.
- Take care to remove any skewers, wires or cocktail sticks used to secure cakes in position before eating.

Credits

Food
Food editor Hannah Yeadon
Food assistant Lottie Covell
Recipes & food styling Sophie Austen-Smith,
Valerie Barrett, Nadine Brown, Sal Henley,
Miranda Keyes, Angela Patel, Angela Romeo
and Mima Sinclair

Design
Art director Nina Christopher
Senior art director David Jenkins
Design Dan Perry

Editorial
Editors Ward Hellewell and Julie Stevens
Editorial assistant Emma Brooke

Account management
Account executive Joanna Brennan
Client director Andy Roughton
Head of content Helen Renshaw

Photography
Photography Michael Hart
Prop stylist Morag Farquhar

For Sainsbury's
Book team Phil Carroll, Mavis Sarfo,
Lynne de Lacy, Lee Scott and Louise Ward
Nutrition Annie Denny

Print & production
Colour origination F1 Colour Ltd
Printers Butler Tanner & Dennis Ltd

Special thanks to...
Francesca Clarke, Lucy Davey and
Clare Devane

© Produced by Seven Publishing on behalf of
Sainsbury's Supermarkets Ltd, 33 Holborn,
London EC1N 2HT. Published February 2014.
All rights reserved. No part of this publication
may be reproduced, stored in a retrieval system or
transmitted in any form by any means, electronic,
mechanical, photocopying, recording or otherwise,
without the prior written permission of Seven
Publishing. Printed and bound by Butler,
Tanner & Dennis Ltd, Frome and London.
ISBN-13: 978-0-9928273-0-4

seven.co.uk

MIX
Paper from
responsible sources
FSC® C023561
www.fsc.org